# COPP
## IN SHOCK

# COPP
# IN SHOCK

*by*

## DON PENDLETON

DONALD I. FINE, INC.
*New York*

Library of Congress Cataloging-in-Publication Data

Pendleton, Don.
Copp in shock / Don Pendleton.
p.   cm.
ISBN 1-55611-287-4
I. Title.
PS3566.E465C654   1992
813'.54—dc20
91-58661
CIP

Manufactured in the United States of America

10   9   8   7   6   5   4   3   2   1

Designed by Irving Perkins Associates

*For my beautiful and courageous wife, Linda—*
*and for my good friends,*
*J. Douglas Halford and Lillie Diamond—*
*who between them brought me through a serious*
*illness and helped me find the words again.*
*This book could not have been possible*
*without their loving support, encouragement*
*and rich humor during a very difficult period.*
*My gratitude forever,*

dp

"Deep into that darkness peering, long I stood there wondering, fearing."

—EDGAR ALLAN POE,
*The Raven*

"For now we see through a glass darkly; but then face to face."

—PAUL
I Corinthians 13:12

"Indecision immobilizes. A cop really has no choice but to step forward out of the darkness and shake hands with fear. A good cop *does* something, right or wrong—even if through a glass darkly—and hopes that he was right."

—JOE COPP
American Private
Investigator

# CHAPTER ONE

**"D**O YOU KNOW who I am?"

The guy kept asking me that question over and over and to tell the truth I wasn't interested in the answer. I'm sure the guy meant well. I wasn't trying to give him a bad time but it just didn't seem to have any relevance.

So I asked him, "Do *you* know who you are?"

He replied, "Let me put it another way. Do you know what my job is?"

He seemed like a nice enough guy, but boy, was he screwed up. He didn't know who he was and he didn't know what his job was. I really didn't want to hurt his feelings, but at this moment I was beginning to get a bit aggravated about all this so I said, "To tell the truth, guy, I'm not real sure right now who I am either, so don't feel bad. What can I do for you?"

This gave the guy a little bit of a chuckle as he replied, "It would be quite a thrill right now if you could just tell me who I am."

Well, that was okay with me, whatever turns you on. "Would it really make your day if I told you you're a dead ringer for Louie XIV?"

"Am I?"

"Not really, but I thought maybe it would liven things a bit for you. What'd you have in mind?"

That gave him another chuckle. "This is University Medical Center and I am Dr. Hansen. Do you know why you are here?"

I said, "Not unless it has something to do with these banshees dancing inside my skull. You're my doctor, huh?"

"Yes, I'm the staff neurologist. But tell me, do you know what a banshee is?"

This guy was loaded with "twenty questions." I told him, "Last I heard, the banshee is a spirit wailing at the approach of death. But don't take that literally, I don't . . . or should I? What's happening with me, Doc?"

He said, "You had a small gunshot wound."

"How small?"

"Bad enough to jangle your head a bit. You have been out of it for the last five days. These are the first coherent words you've given me since you came in here. Do you understand what has happened to you?"

Suddenly this gave me an almost overpowering sense of inexplicable sadness. "Not really," I replied. "What is going on with my head?"

"You had a severe concussion, and also lost quite a bit of blood, but you got off easier than it may feel to you right now. No vital damage—you were just grazed by that bullet—it's the concussion and some brain swelling that has given you most of the problem. That could be causing you some confusion, but it will pass. You could be out of here in a few days—as soon as your confusion clears up."

That sounded like good news to me except that I really

didn't feel all that confused. Of course I had no memory of being shot and knew nothing about any of that. A crazy thought occurred to me at about that moment. I asked the doctor, "Do you know who I am?"

The doctor showed me a startled look and replied, "Can't you answer that question for yourself?"

"Maybe, but I asked you first."

"Do you have some confusion about that?"

"You're the one who's asking all the questions. Are you confused, Doc?"

That was good for another laugh. "We can settle the question real easy. What is your name?"

As a matter of fact, I was not sure that I could answer that. It was not that I did not know my own name, but it was just as though my mind was playing games with me and couldn't quite come up with the answer. I knew the answer, of course, it was just eluding me for a moment. I know that I wasn't hitting on all my cylinders, but I kept expecting all that to come into focus and it just wasn't doing so. It is weird when you feel as if you need to look into a mirror to remember who you are, and let me tell you, it scares the shit out of you to realize that you might look into that mirror and not even recognize the face gazing back. And that is about where I was at.

I told the doctor, "Sure I know my own name and it will come to me in just a second. Who tried to snuff me?"

"Sorry, Joe, that's out of my field. Don't you know who shot you?"

No, I did not know at the moment who shot me, but the Doc had just given me the clue I had been searching for. It was like stepping out of the darkness into a sunlit day. "I'm Joe Copp," I told him. "I'm a private eye. I've got to get out of here. Where are my clothes?"

I tried to get out of bed and almost fell on my face. Dr. Hansen gently wrestled me back onto the bed and said, "Not so fast, Joe. One step at a time. We need to get you a little stronger and your head a bit clearer before you go dancing out of here."

Hansen was really a nice guy and obviously he was trying to help me, but I needed to get my own head back together. I was glad when he went away and left me alone. I wanted to get a look into a mirror and see for myself what was happening with me. That was a mistake. I didn't like what I saw in the mirror. There was a bandage twisted about the right side of my head that looked ominous as hell, also some small scratches along the bridge of the nose. Someone with no barbering skills had given me a lousy haircut, exposing naked scalp around the bandaged area, taking my sideburn with it. I could handle that, no big deal except that it just didn't look like me. What I was having trouble with was that I didn't feel like myself. I felt clumsy, confused, detached; everything had a sense of unreality. I guess what I am trying to say is that I did not feel threatened or challenged by any of this, almost as though it really didn't matter, and that is just not like me. I am not sure that I knew who Joe Copp really was, and the strange thing is, I think that a part of me didn't even care about that.

Even so, I think I was having something like an identity crisis at some unconscious level that only surfaced now and then.

Two homicide cops showed up while I was engrossed in that introspection. I did not feel like talking to those guys. I was still buzzing a little in the head and not at all sure that I could handle an intelligent conversation with them.

I had known one of these guys in the past so it was not a totally cold interview. They were polite and maybe even a bit sympathetic about my situation. I had worked with Bill Andrews shortly before I left the Sheriff's Department and went into business for myself as a private cop. I had not known Tony Zambrano but apparently the guy had heard stories about me and seemed friendly enough. I had no reason to be coy with these two; I was just having trouble recalling the incident.

Andrews asked me, "Who pulled the trigger on you, Joe?"

I told him, "This is going to sound weird, but all I know about it is what the doctor told me, which is next to nothing. I'm hoping that you guys can help me with that."

Andrews replied, "All we know is that you called 911 and asked for help."

"Where was that?"

"Your pad."

Zambrano added, "Your place was a mess, Joe. Blood all over the place. Where's your gun?"

"Hell, I don't know. I don't usually carry a piece unless I'm working. Maybe it's here. Check my personal belongings."

Zambrano said, "It's not here, Joe. Where do you think it might be?"

"Must be at home then—or maybe it's in my car."

"Not there either," Andrews said. "It'll turn up. What do you know about Martha Kaufman?"

"Don't think I know the lady," I told him. "Is it important?"

Andrews replied, "Could be. The name rings no bells for you?"

"Not for me. Is she pretty?"

"Maybe she was—until someone blew her apart with a Smith & Wesson .41 Mag."

I said, "That's a rare piece. That's what I carry."

Andrews replied, "Yeah."

I said, "Wait a minute—that's why Zambrano asked about my . . . "

"Yeah."

I said, "Oh, shit. Are you guys trying to tell me it was my gun . . . "

Andrews told me, "Not officially, Joe. But you'd better get your act together here, and quick—the D.A. may not be as sympathetic with your situation as we have been."

"Thanks," I said. "I'll straighten this out as soon as I get my head back together."

"Do it quick, Joe," Andrews said quietly.

The two deputies gave me restrained smiles and walked out.

So what the hell did all this mean? I have played these same games myself during a police investigation so I knew that those two had not been toying with me despite all the friendly smiles and soft words. These guys were conducting a homicide investigation, no question about it, and they had come to just pass the time of day with me. The warning from Bill Andrews was clear and to the point. Apparently I was in trouble and it seemed that I didn't even know why. But that was a friendly warning from Andrews and I would be a fool to disregard it. I had to get out of that place and put my mind back together my own way and in my own time. Which meant that I had to do it right now.

I got dressed and was slipping into my shoes when this six-foot-five black orderly came into my room. He shot me a look of surprise and said, "What you doing, man?"

"I'm getting into my clothes," I told him. "Do you have a problem with that?"

"They're not mine. But look at you, man, you're falling all over yourself. Are you sure you know what you're doing?"

I told him, "No, but I've got to get out of here, I have a hot date. How do I get out of this place?"

The orderly said, "You can't even walk, man. Come on, get back in bed."

I told him, "You're a Brother. I'm in deep trouble. Help me find a taxi...or show me the way out of here."

"It's my job, man. You trying to screw me up."

"No, Brother. It may be your job, but it's my life that's on the line."

The big black man was having a problem with this. He said, "It's your ass, man. Second door on the right, take the stairs. Shit—you'll never make it."

"I'll make it," I assured him. "What's your name? I'll make this up to you."

The black man said, "Shit," with a disgusted look and took me by the hand. He practically carried me down the stairs and bundled me carefully into the backseat of an idling taxi. I'm no lightweight myself; I tip in at about two-sixty, with a height of six-three, but this guy was handling me as if I were a baby. "Good luck," he said gruffly.

His name was James Jefferson. I caught it from his name tag as he was tucking me into the taxi. "Thank you, James. I'll be getting back to you."

"Shit," he said and hurried away.

I meant it, though, and I would not forget James Jefferson. I think maybe he saved my life.

# CHAPTER TWO

I T WAS MY house, okay, but somehow it just didn't seem the same. The lawn hadn't been mowed recently and the whole place looked a little seedy. It had been my pride and joy since the day I first took possession of the property and it had never looked this bad. My old Cad was parked askew in the driveway with a flat tire and a shattered windshield. I knew I would not have allowed this to have gone unattended. So what the hell had been going on here? This was just not Joe Copp's style. I have never allowed things to go to hell. Some of the guys at the department used to joke about what a great house-wife I had become, but what the hell, there was a big investment in this place, and probably the only house I would ever own. After leaving the department, there were many woolly days when I wondered if I would be able to meet those hefty mortgage payments, but it has always been my number-one priority and somehow I have managed since being on my own as a freelance P.I.

I had to go inside the house to get some money to pay the cabby but I didn't have my keys, which was no big deal, because I had always kept a cheater key stashed near my back door, which opens into my office. I grabbed some cash from my office safe and took care of the cabby.

As strange as it may sound, I could not stand the idea of my old Cad sitting in the driveway wounded. The Cad was a fully paid-off Eldorado gas guzzler, and in a sentimental way it was my pride and joy. It had saved my life on several occasions and I didn't like the idea of it being busted up like that. We'd been through a lot together and maybe we'd be through a lot yet. I couldn't just leave it there to die. I got on the horn and called my old friend, Leonard, who wields mechanical tools like a Michelangelo. No repair is beyond his artistry.

Once back inside, the realization hit me of just how badly I had been hurt. My blood was all over the place. Apparently I had been staggering around in a daze trying to put myself back together. I guess I had bounced around the house quite a bit before I realized that I needed help because the evidence of my struggle was everywhere; the telephone was blood-caked, a pile of soiled towels lay in the bathroom, several pieces of furniture were overturned, and it seemed obvious that it had taken a hell of an effort to keep myself functioning long enough to connect with the 911 operator for help.

I knew in order to get into this case I had to make myself presentable. I peeled off the bandage and winced at the mess someone had made of my head. I resolved I would have to do something about my appearance if I were going to be effective. There was only one person I could think of who could help me with that. I called my pal, Molly, and locked in a quick appointment for some window dressing. She had been a buddy of mine since the time we were neighbors in the small shopping center complex where my office had been situated until recently.

I drove my van down the hill to Molly's beauty shop. She greeted me with her usual warm smile and the standard cup of hot coffee. "You look like hell, Joe. What have you done with yourself this time?"

I knew she was right. I did look like hell. "Would you believe that I'm not sure? Think you could patch up this damaged piece of shit and make it look presentable?"

"I'm just a hairdresser, Joe, I don't do plastic surgery or divine healing. But I'd be glad to work on any other body parts ailing you."

"I'm afraid the parts you might find the most interesting may not be working up to par. How about a rain check? Right now I'd feel fine if you could bring back the real Joe Copp." The sexual banter had been a running gag between us for years. But one of these days I might call her bluff and scare the hell out of her.

Molly said, "Well then, let's get this show on the road and get to work on your par game."

She ushered me back to the alcove in the rear of the shop and gingerly went to work on my bandage. She gently lifted off the gauze pads, exposing the mess underneath, and asked me, "Do you really want to look at this, Joe?"

"Does it look that bad to you?"

"I wouldn't want to kiss it, Joe. How can you not remember this!"

I replied soberly, "Lots of things I'm not remembering right now, Molly."

"Maybe that's for the best right now. What do you want me to do with this mess?"

"Just make me look pretty."

"I don't think it's possible to make you pretty, love,

but would you settle for the same old Joe?"

"If that's the best you can do, okay. Just don't make me fatally attractive."

"You came in with the fatal part, I'll supply the attractive part, then I'm going to jump your bones, Joe."

I still wondered sometimes if Molly was really kidding about all the lust 'n love talk. But it was no time to be exploring ideas like that. I had too many other unanswered questions percolating through my traumatized brain and I still knew that I must stay one step ahead of the cops until I got myself back together.

Molly performed her usual magic, added a thin adhesive strip and patched some wig fragments over the wounded area. I appeared almost normal and I figured one of the hats in my closet would finish off the look. At least now I wouldn't be scaring little children on the street.

I gave Molly a warm hug and a quick kiss and I carefully found my way back into the van. I was still feeling a bit woozy, not dizzy exactly, but maybe a bit unsure of my navigational skills. I needed to get back home and start to unravel the mysteries that were clouding my mind. Someone tried to blow me away and it was time to find out who . . . and why. There was a strong probability that the cops were considering hanging a murder rap on me and I had to find out if there was any connection between my own shooting and the woman's murder.

My place is in the foothills overlooking the San Gabriel Valley, about thirty miles east of the L.A. civic center. It's on semi-isolated acreage of horse estates dotted with shrubbery and trees. Most of my neighbors place big store in the fact that there is room for horses and plenty of privacy, the kind of place where people mind their own and expect the same of others. The horses are no attraction for me but the ever-persistent flies seem to love them.

In the truest sense, my home is my castle. I have a theory that our homes reveal who we are and what we think of ourselves. A lot of people seem to believe that they find themselves in their work or play. I believe that you find yourself where you live, because that is the only place where you truly are yourself.

I turned off the main road onto the lane leading up to my house and I was relieved to see that Leonard was on his job and had taken the Cad for repair.

I let myself in through my prized Grecian entryway, a sort of a mini-colonnade floored with Italian tile lifting to a reception hall. Off to the left and down is the kitchen and utility space; off to the right and up is the living room; a single large bedroom takes up the whole back of the house. I've got a spa back there, a small workout gym, and my business entrance is via the patio door, which opens directly into a partitioned office area just in case it would be a little unsettling for my clients to invade my bedroom.

The first thing that struck me as I stepped inside was a painting hanging on the wall above the couch in the living room. Funny, I hadn't noticed it before. It was large and looked more expensive than I knew I could afford, so what was it doing in my house? Something about the painting gave me a shivery feeling, almost like a foreboding. In spite of my unease, I had a feeling for the painting; it was a glorious pastoral scene of the high country. I pulled it off the wall for a closer look, disturbed that I seemed to be seeing it for the first time, and I had to wonder what else had been erased from my memory by that bullet.

The indistinguishable artist's signature told me nothing, but a small sticker on the back of the painting identified the Kaufman Gallery, Mammoth Lakes, California, and the title "God's Country." As I was returning it to its place on the wall, there was a reoccurrence of the inexplicable sadness that had gripped me earlier in the hospital. It was just a momentary flash and I really didn't understand it, but I knew that it meant something important because I found myself tearing, and I don't cry easily.

I had to soak this one through so I heated up the spa and immersed myself for a long one. I knew that I was pretty badly scrambled, almost as if the left brain was not hooking up with the right brain. I was in obvious confusion and that is a hell of a scary place to be when your life may be on the line. What was it the homicide detective said to me? . . . did he say Kaufman—dammit! The painting was labeled . . . oh shit, Kaufman Gallery. Mammoth, yeah, but why Mammoth? I was sure that I had not been there in years. I used to do a bit of trout fishing there but it's been ages, I thought. If I had been there recently and didn't even know it, then I was truly screwed up.

I came quickly out of the tub, soaking wet and bucknaked, and took another look at that painting. Dammit—the goddamned tears again—what the hell?

I went without pause to the telephone and called Johnnie Chen, my forensics man at the county morgue. He confirmed that there was an unclaimed female gunshot victim by the name of Kaufman and that was all he knew about her, which didn't help a hell of a lot.

I was going to have to take a look at this victim for myself even though something inside of me said, "Don't go, Joe."

But I had to go. I had to know.

I toweled off, dressed, and began rummaging through my papers in the office safe. I found a receipt for the "God's Country" painting. I had paid nineteen hundred dollars for it! I could hardly see myself paying that kind of money for a painting unless I had suddenly struck it rich, and I didn't see any evidence of that. I characteristically keep very detailed business records and my ledger revealed two trips to Mammoth recently. What the hell had I been into that may have resulted in a woman's death? It appeared that I would have to return to Mammoth with hope that I could bring the shattered memories into focus. Maybe my life depended on it.

I KNEW I shouldn't have gone. Death in the morgue is never a pretty sight, but this was even more unsettling than usual. Clearly, she had been a very pretty woman. She had stood about five foot ten and was very nicely put together before two big slugs changed all that. In spite of the gruesome disfiguration of the body, I knew in my gut that I had known this woman and that I had known her intimately even though it was a very fuzzy recollection. If I had known her well enough to have been somehow involved in her death, then at least I needed to involve myself in her life. The only way I knew how to do that was to discover the truth about Mammoth.

I had to go.

# CHAPTER THREE

MAMMOTH LAKES IS beautifully nestled in the eastern High Sierra Nevadas about six hours northeast of the L.A. basin and about three hours south of the Lake Tahoe, California–Nevada line. It's a small mountain community that has long been a popular resort area for both winter and summer sports. The long drive across the Mojave desert is largely uninteresting, until suddenly you encounter Mt. Whitney, the highest mountain peak in the contiguous United States. At this point the wild, rugged beauty of the mountains is almost seductive in its natural splendor, and the dramatic moonlit view was actually therapeutic for me.

As I approached the mountain community of Bishop, less than an hour from Mammoth, it was nearing midnight. My brain was working overtime and I was feeling jangled and out of sorts so I took a motel room for the night as it didn't make a lot of sense to push on to Mammoth at this hour. Besides, I wanted to hit the place fresh and in the daylight.

I was up and rolling at six o'clock and wheeled the van off U.S. 395 at the junction with the Mammoth Lakes road shortly before seven. As I came into town I was startled at how familiar it all looked in spite of the fact that I had no memory of being there for at least ten years. It did not really leap at me until a seemingly new McDonald's restaurant came into view. The architecture was rustic and unlike the classical McDonald's layout. I *knew* that I had been in that particular restaurant before; I almost missed it.

While inside, nursing a coffee, one of Mammoth's finest strode past, gave me a little half smile, and said, "The mighty Joe Copp. How's it going, Joe?"

I didn't know this guy from Adam but he seemed pleasant enough despite the almost sneering remark. I called him back, and asked, "You know me, pal?"

"Do I *know* you! It took four of us to take you down when you were busting up the Kaufman Gallery."

"When was that?"

"Short memory, Joe? I'll never forget it."

"Sorry about that. Nothing personal intended. How'd I do?"

"You did better than the boys from Tahoe. They'll never get over it. I like your style, Joe."

The cop gave me an amiable wave and went on out. So what the hell did I have here now? What boys from Tahoe? So obviously I had been to that gallery and I even got into a beef. Could it have been enough to get a girl killed? Evidently there was no connection in this town yet between the Kaufman Gallery and the dead girl in Los Angeles. I needed to go check out the gallery as my first item of business although I still seemed to have a lot of resistance to the very idea, but I was hoping the visit would shake up my memory banks and shed some light on my connection with the place.

Think again, Joe—the Kaufman Gallery was no more.

The place had been gutted by fire, and fairly recently, it seemed.

A couple of workmen were tearing away the dead timber and the whole place was a charred mess. I had to go inside and give it a look even though just the sight of the place was enough to confirm my growing feeling that something terrible and dark had happened here.

As I stepped inside the rubble one of the workmen approached and said to me, "Are you the insurance man?"

I replied, "Just an interested friend. What the hell happened here?"

"The fire marshal is calling it arson."

"When?"

"About a week ago. Damn shame, it was a beautiful place. Wonder how Martha's taking it."

That comment was like a bolt of lightning zapping me. It was the same feeling I had been getting every time I encountered her name—an indescribable sadness and sense of loss. I did not trust myself to respond to that question. My ears were ringing and I felt dizzy, a bit disoriented. I guess I mumbled something in reply but I have no idea of what I might have said. Apparently I made no sense to him because he just stared at me as I stumbled away and beat it out of there.

I guess I was in worse shape than I realized. It was not my style to back away from the truth and I knew that was exactly what I was doing, and I didn't like it. But what could be so terrible about the truth? So, a woman was dead. That can never be a happy event but I have managed to live through it many times in the past so what was so different about this one? I'm not a total dummy. Evidently I was responsible in some way and that was why my head was so scrambled. I didn't know because I didn't want to know and I didn't want to know probably because I was somehow responsible for this woman's death. Enough of this idle speculation. It was time to get back on track and quit feeling sorry for myself.

I checked my notes and drove over to the hotel, where my records showed that I had recently spent time. It was just a few blocks from the heart of town, an upscale inn that looked fairly new, maybe a bit familiar, but it did not stir any particular memory when I went inside. The desk clerk seemed to recognize me though, showed me a cheery smile, and said, "Nice to see you back. What can I do for you?"

She was a pretty girl of about twenty-five with fiery red hair and interesting green eyes. I did not want to tell her that she was a total stranger to me, just in case she wasn't. I'm sure that I would have wanted to get to know her better—and for all I knew, maybe I had. I spotted her name on the breast pocket of her uniform and replied, "Hi, Cindy. Think I need a room for a day or so. Can you take care of me?"

She gave me a startled look and even seemed a bit embarrassed as she replied, "Things not going well with you and Martha?"

Martha again. Jesus. We must have really been an item up here. I said, rather lamely, "She went to L.A."

Cindy said, "Oh," in obvious confusion but covered it quickly. "Sure, we have room for you. That will be a single room?"

"For now, yeah."

There was a noticeable chill in the air at this point. I turned over my credit card and signed the registration. She gave me my room key without further comment. Either she was still feeling some embarrassment or there was something personal between the two of us that had her a bit on edge and noticeably distant. Whatever, that was the end of our conversation. I pocketed my key and went directly to the phone bank across the lobby, scored instantly with a listing for M. Kaufman on Old Mammoth Road.

I found it to be a small condo complex at the edge of town, a short drive from the hotel. Condominiums have truly come into their own in this region. It seems to be the major choice for housing, primarily alpine-mountain architecture, emphasizing an aesthetic blending with the environment. Mammoth has a stable permanent population of five thousand, with probably two to three times that number at the peak tourist seasons.

I didn't have to use my burglary skills to get inside because some subliminal sense moved me straight to the hidden key buried in a planter at the front door. It looked so familiar, I really didn't feel like a second-story man. The feeling of déjà vu intensified as I stepped inside. I think I would have been disappointed to have found a conventional setting with no charm or character. Her special touches were evident everywhere, with artistic and even dramatic style and grace.

This had the same feeling as my own place, and in particular it produced the same appreciation that I had found in the painting of "God's Country" now hanging in my living room. This was a special woman, one that I would have enjoyed spending time with. The weirdest part was when I found my own shaving gear in the bathroom and some of my own clothing on hangers in the bedroom closet. Then I noticed the photograph on the nightstand beside the bed. It was of Martha Kaufman and me, a Polaroid, the type snapped by roving casino photographers. Hell, I had been living with her! My god! This could not have been a casual relationship! I knew her intimately! And I was getting solid evidence of that truth as I began experiencing these same overwhelming feelings that had been flashing on me in an almost subliminal level ever since I hit town.

It was almost too intense to stay in there. I sat down on the bed and tried to pull myself together but the tears came anyway—a grief like I had never experienced. What the hell—this wasn't like tough Joe Copp. So what was going down with me? I had the feeling that somehow I had betrayed her. I began to feel tainted and dirty inside, almost as though I had been directly responsible for this beautiful woman's death.

Okay, Joe, wake up! Start thinking like a cop, dammit! The woman is dead. I almost got it, too. Okay—there was a brawl in her gallery . . . two guys from Tahoe making trouble for her . . . it seems that I bought a piece of that action . . . the police intervened. Why were thugs from Tahoe coming down on this obviously cultured woman? Could this have been the catalyst that produced a deadly encounter in Los Angeles?

This was almost terrifying but I knew I had to break through into the truth, which was banging at me. Nothing could be worse than this confusion. It was hurting like hell but I knew that I had to move with this photograph. There was nothing ordinary about this woman.

Her dramatic dark eyes almost hypnotically pulled me into the picture. A classical, statuesque woman of about thirty with soft brown hair worn rather casually, very pretty, strong with a sense of self coupled with a soft and almost wistful vulnerability. She dressed well but not flamboyantly. She was an artisan, a dreamer, an achiever.

I was falling in love with her...for the second time, it seemed.

But enough of this. I needed to get to work. The cop at McDonald's made me feel almost like a local celebrity, so maybe I could get something from these people. I used Martha's telephone to call Mammoth P.D. The woman at the switchboard seemed to recognize my name, too, and switched me instantly to Chief Terry. That was a surprise, but Terry seemed interested and cooperative.

"Joe, how's it going? One of my boys mentioned that you're back in town. Big-city boys treating you okay?"

"Not really. I'll tell you all about it when I come in. Right now, I need to get a copy of your report on my incident at the gallery with those guys from Tahoe. Also, whatever you have on the fire. I'd appreciate it, Chief."

"No problem. When do you want to pick it up?"

"How about an hour. Would that squeeze you too close?"

"You got it, bud. Don't cut it so close that we can't stop and chat awhile."

I thanked him and began feeling like a cop again. The brief conversation somehow had the effect of clearing my head a bit. I went into the kitchen and rummaged through the refrigerator and cupboards just looking for a sensing of the place. I found a six-pack of my favorite beer and various goodies; it seemed that at least once we had walked the aisles of the supermarket together.

I hit real pay dirt in a cabinet in the living room. It was a shocker, and it damn near carried me over the edge.

I found a marriage certificate in that cabinet.

I had married Martha Lynn Kaufman in Tahoe shortly before the shooting in L.A.

*I had failed to prevent the murder of my own bride!*
And now I was really in shock!

# CHAPTER FOUR

I T HAD BEEN a whirlwind romance. I knew that much, now, and I was remembering it in bits and slices. It had really started when two guys began pushing her around in the gallery and I went to her assistance. That part was clear and firmly etched into my awareness. It was our first meeting and I recall hanging around and browsing through the artworks waiting for an opportunity to introduce myself. The two guys from Tahoe came in and began throwing their weight around before I had a chance even to speak to her. One thing followed another and I ended up tossing those guys into the street before I even knew her name. As fate would have it, that incident was what brought us together. I remembered then our first conversation and her warm appreciation for my effort. She had been strongly unnerved by the incident and she invited me next door for a cappuccino and Danish.

I was in love with her before the second cappuccino.

When we returned to the gallery, she knew that I had been drawn to the "God's Country" painting and she tried to give it to me as a gift. I could not accept such a valuable painting scot-free so we compromised and I took it at her cost. Dinner for two at seven o'clock was included in the deal.

That dinner lasted until midnight and obviously neither of us wanted it to end. We went to her place and talked into the wee hours. The sun was breaking over the mountains when I finally tore myself away and reluctantly said good night.

I arrived at the hotel too wired to get right to sleep. I must have lain there for an hour or more before finally nodding off, and then it seemed I dreamed of her continuously until I awoke at noon. I called her at the gallery before I even got out of bed—showered and shaved, got into some fresh clothes, and was at her door a half hour later.

I walked in and we stared at each other; there was no need for words. She went to the front window and put up the CLOSED sign. She turned back to me and said softly, "What do you have in mind?"

"What do you have on tap?"

"I do a mean Eggs Benedict. How does that sound?"

"Sounds great."

I followed her in my van to her condo, just a few minutes from the gallery.

She did do a mean Eggs Benedict but that wasn't the chief attraction of the moment. I couldn't keep my eyes off her and obviously neither of us was all that interested in the food. I helped her with the kitchen clean-up and we both knew what was next. We looked at each other with the same mind. I picked her up and carried her into the bedroom and not another word was spoken until we lay naked together and she gasped, "Oh God, Joe. I never knew that I could feel this way."

I told her, "Me neither. And, God, I never want to feel any other way again!"

It was the sweetest passion I had ever known and, at the same time, the wildest and most uninhibited hunger I could ever imagine expressed between a civilized man and woman.

The pain of reliving that memory was not as traumatic as one might think. In fact, the remembrance was actually clearing my mind. It was almost like a healing even though it was probably as poignant a pain as I had ever experienced. I still did not have all the answers, of course, but the big picture was coming into focus rapidly, and somehow it was far better this way no matter how brutal the truth. I still had to deal with the terrible feelings of guilt, pain, and anger, but at least it was making me feel like a cop again and I knew that my only way through this confusion was to deal with it head-on. It would not come in a single leap, of course, but simply knowing the truth, no matter how painful that may be, was far better than this ringing confusion that had been my constant companion since awakening in the hospital. It had never been my style to shun the truth, no matter how unnerving; I could not expect to find honest comfort any other way.

It was time to keep my appointment with the Chief, John Terry. He was waiting for me in his office and gave me a warm greeting. I remembered this guy—a prematurely gray six-footer, a deceptively laid-back guy who I knew could stomp ass—and quickly—when the occasion arose. He was a no-crap square shooter, and I liked him. It seemed almost like greeting an old friend though I'm sure we hadn't spent that much time together. I had a sudden image of this guy riding me like a Brahma bull during the scuffle at the Kaufman Gallery, doing his best to keep the peace in his small town. I can admire a guy like this and obviously we had much in common.

"Are you working on something, Joe?" the Chief asked as he slid the reports across the desk at me.

I said, "Trying to. Is it your feeling that someone torched the Kaufman Gallery?"

He replied, "Yeah, no question about it. Has the marks of a professional job. It was quick and it was thorough. Those guys knew what they were doing."

I asked him, "Do you sense a connection to the fight at the gallery?"

"Seems to figure. What do you think?"

"Do bears shit in the woods?"

Chief Terry replied, "Sure. Even in Nevada. I have included their rap sheets in the report. But our people in Tahoe tell me they've gone south."

"How far south?"

"These thugs are L.A. muscle and they are *connected.* A ream of rap sheets but no convictions. Like homing pigeons, these two have an instinct for survival and I'd guess L.A. is where we would find them."

"Have you been trying to find them?"

"For what? We have no wants on them."

I said to him, "You'd love to nail them, though, wouldn't you?"

The Chief replied, "I'd only give about a month's pay for a shot like that."

I said, "Maybe we can make it cheaper than that."

There was a long pause before the Chief responded.

"You sound troubled, Joe. What's bothering you? What are you hiding under that hat?"

"There is plenty I haven't told you yet."

Terry leaned over for a closer look as I removed my hat. He whistled. "Is that as mean as it looks?"

I replied, "I caught a bullet. One more silly millimeter and I wouldn't be here talking about it. I've been on my back for a week. I still have birdies in my belfry if I move too quick."

We stared at each other silently for a moment, then he asked, "What else are you keeping from me, Joe?"

"Martha is dead," I told him quietly. "She was killed in Los Angeles last week. It's still a little fuzzy in my mind at this point. I didn't even know my own name until yesterday. I know this much—she was scared, and I was scared, and I was trying to get her to a safe place. I failed. Martha didn't make it. God, John, I wish I hadn't made it. I have been going crazy with this. I've been lying in her bed all morning just trying to get my head together."

The Chief said, in a barely audible voice, "Christ, Joe, I'm sorry. This is heavy shit. God! She was too good for this. I've known her most of her life. It's tearing me up too. You two looked so right together. Jesus, Joe. I'm sorry."

"Did you know that we were married ten days ago in Tahoe?"

"Jesus!"

Some guys you just know even before you know them. He was sincerely shaken by this news. John Terry was a cop with heart. You don't always find that in the dehumanizing pressures of police work. I liked this guy and I felt a bond despite the often conflicting interests that naturally arise between the private and public cop. There seemed to be none of this crap between us and he was obviously sharing my pain over Martha's death.

I had to level with him all the way. "The L.A. Sheriff's Department told me that she was killed with my gun. I think they're trying to connect me to the shooting. At the moment I have no direct memory of her death. It was really strange when I went to the morgue to view her body. She was a total stranger; it was like seeing her for the first time. My memory of us together didn't really start coming back until a few hours ago. Now it's driving me crazy. I came up here to try and put the pieces of the puzzle together in the hope that I could stay a step ahead of their investigation."

"Were you and Martha shot at the same time?"

"Dammit, Chief, that's what's driving me crazy. I don't know what happened. It's starting to come back in pieces, but I don't have a clear picture of any of it yet. I was worried about her and I was taking her away from here, that's all I know for sure, but I believe someone jumped us on the way to my place near L.A." Terry was giving me a strange look. I said, "You're not really buying all this, are you?"

He replied, "Let's take it a step at a time. It does sound a bit farfetched, but I have to go with you on this, at least for the moment. Thanks for being square with me, Joe. How can I help?"

"This may sound crazy but I know nothing about Martha. Can you give me a bit of her background?"

The Chief was still a little bowled over by all this. He said, "Are you serious? You didn't know that she was Harley Sanford's kid?"

"Who is Sanford?"

"God, you are screwed up. He's just the biggest man in this area. Construction, development, banking, he's into all of it—even some of the Tahoe gambling action. Has a lake house up there. Hell, he's got homes in three counties."

"Is he clean?"

"You hear things, you know, but guys like Sanford are always in the spotlight and who can guess what's truth and what's envy. So far as I've ever heard, he's always been clean. Mrs. Sanford is a real stand-up lady, I can tell you that much." After a short pause, Terry asked me, "Did you know about George Kaufman?"

I replied, "Not that I remember."

"She was married to him, Joe."

"She, who?"

"Martha, dammit. You're really serious—you didn't know about any of this? Kaufman worked for the old man. Martha married him about five years ago."

"So where is he now?"

"He was killed in a car accident up near Tahoe a couple years ago. I gather that it was not a particularly happy marriage. If memory serves me right, they were in the process of divorcing when he died. He was in with some fast company up there, and to tell you the truth, I've always wondered about that 'accident.' Have you I.D.'d her to the L.A. authorities?"

"Not yet."

"I'll take care of those details. Poor bastard, you must be in shock over this. After I've confirmed it, would you like for me to notify the family?"

"Jesus, that sounds so cold. I haven't even met the family...I guess. Maybe I should go over there."

"Would you like it if I went with you?"

I said, "I'd appreciate that, Chief. I'm still a bit numb about all this."

"I think it best I go along. You're in for some surprises with this family. Why don't you meet me back here in an hour. I'll get on the horn with L.A. and get all the facts I can. Harley Sanford is going to want to know all the gory details. He's a man accustomed to getting his way. You might be in for a rough time there, Joe."

I thanked the Chief and stumbled out of there feeling crippled, blind and half crazy, realizing that the more I learned the less I knew. It was something like going at a Chinese puzzle with a chain saw, blindfolded and handcuffed; the closer you get, the more dangerous it becomes. Except this was not just a game—it was probably for the whole enchilada. It felt like I was taking a blind plunge into a devastating abyss that would totally engulf me.

Okay—if so, let it be.

I had to do what I had to do.

# CHAPTER FIVE

KNEW THAT I had to have been crazy in love with this woman because I had bowed out of the marriage game after too many false starts during an eighteen-year police career. Cops should never get married, and I had learned that truth the hard way. There had to have been something very special about Martha for me to even consider another tussle with that kind of record. My former wives had been good women; it wasn't their failure that we couldn't hold it together. It was my failure. It seemed that the work always came first, and you can't expect any woman to play second fiddle to that kind of commitment. Maybe what it amounted to, for me, is that I always *wanted* the work to come first. No woman wants to be the second choice in any man's life.

The more I learned about Martha Kaufman, the more I understood how I could have fallen head over heels in love and married her. I had sworn, "Never again," but obviously she had become the beautiful exception to my rule. Now her mystique was enveloping me, drawing me into her as if she were still alive. She had come, and it was beautiful, but now she was gone. I was alive. I had to go on living with the cards I had drawn. For sure I had to get myself together enough to find the creeps who killed her. I could not bring her back, but I owed her justice. It was the least I could do.

I still felt drawn to a dead woman and I wanted to have another go at that condo. It seemed senseless to be paying for a hotel room I did not need, so I first ran past the hotel and canceled the room I had taken. Cindy, the desk clerk, still seemed a bit stiff with me but she wouldn't hear of keeping my money. She destroyed the charge slip and told me, "If you change your mind, just give me a call."

I said, "Sure, thanks."

I felt impelled to return to Martha's place even though I was meeting Chief Terry in less than an hour. I had been distracted from my search of the apartment by the discovery of our marriage license. I didn't know what I expected to find there, maybe it was just a compulsion to be near her.

I'm glad I went. Two guys surprised me inside her apartment. They had been tearing the place apart in a wild search for God-knows-what. I had a hunch it was the two guys I had tumbled with at the gallery. They both looked scared as hell when I barged in. I said, "Well, well, we keep meeting this way. Which window do you want to be tossed out of this time?"

They seemed to be torn between a fight or flight. I was one short step ahead of their decision. The younger one, a punk of about twenty-five, made the first break. He went for his piece. He didn't get there. I hit him with a smash to the chops and he went down without a murmur. The older guy gave me a sick look and went for his gun. I closed on him with a quick spin and kicked the gun loose and it skittered under the couch. The poor guy didn't know whether to shit or go blind. He had to get past me to retrieve his gun and he clearly had no wish to risk that challenge.

He said, "Can't we talk this over?"

I had to kick the young one down again, and this time I relieved him of his snub-nosed .38. I held it loosely in one hand and said, for the benefit of both, "No games this time, boys. It's time to get serious. Do I shoot your kneecaps off or do we get friendly?"

The young punk was whining and nursing his chops; didn't really feel much like talking. The other guy said, "I think we can straighten this out. There's been a big mistake here. I'm sorry if we startled you. Can we start all over again?"

I told him, "Too weak, pal. You can do better than that. You torched the gallery, you blew the lady away, you tried to blow me away—now you want to be friends. Go get fucked. Give me a reason for not wanting to blow you away."

"You've got it wrong. Why don't you talk this over with Harley Sanford before you do something you might regret?"

"The only thing I might regret, asshole, is that I blow you away too easy. But just for the sake of conversation, why would I have anything to say to Sanford?"

"We work for Mr. Sanford. He sent us over here to collect a few personal items from his daughter."

"Which daughter is that?"

"Martha, the one who owns the gallery. This is her apartment. She's been out of town and he has been missing some of his personal papers, thought maybe we could find them."

I said, "You just don't want to get serious, do you?" I pulled his face into the snout of the .38. "Last chance, pal, try again."

The guy was in a cold sweat. The kid groaned. I had to kick him again to keep his mind on business. The older man said, with an almost desperate plea, "Look, it's not like you seem to think. This is just a routine go-fer job for us. We got no stake in any of this. We haven't blown anybody away and I don't know anything about a torch job. Look—I know your reputation. I wouldn't be playing games at a time like this. You gotta believe me. At least call Mr. Sanford and let's get this straightened out before somebody really gets hurt. Okay?"

I said, "So, okay. Call him."

The relief in that worried mind was obvious. The guy almost leaped for the phone. His hand was shaking as it closed on the handset. I noticed that he did not need to paw through a directory. He had called this number many times. I snatched it away from him at the first ring. A man with an authoritative voice responded.

"Sanford here."

I said, "Copp here. Did you send a couple of boys to smash up your daughter's apartment?"

He replied without hesitation, "Who the hell is this?"

"I gave you the name. I'm Joe Copp. Did you send somebody to break into your daughter's apartment, or didn't you? Let's keep it straight if you have any interest in keeping these guys out of jail."

The harsh voice on the other end asked me, "What's your interest?"

I decided while I was here that I might as well go for

a sensing of this guy. I said, "Martha is my interest. A couple of guys came into her place and began busting it up. They say you sent them. Did you send them?"

Sanford replied, "Did you say the name was Copp? Are you the guy who was involved in that little scuffle at the gallery a couple of weeks ago?"

I told him, "That's me. Are these the same guys?"

He replied, "Do these guys have names?"

I held the receiver over and called out, "He wants your names."

The guy called back, "Mr. Sanford, it's Sammy. This guy's a maniac. Tell him we're okay."

I took the phone back. "Know this guy, Harley?"

Sanford replied, "Yeah, I know him. He's a loyal employee. What's the problem there?"

This guy was smooth as silk. Father-in-law or not, I didn't like this guy. I said, "No problem—thanks," and hung up.

The little punk pulled himself up from the floor and the other guy audibly wheezed with relief. They started for the door, thinking it was over.

"Clean it up," I commanded with a wave of the piece. They literally stopped in their tracks.

"No problem, sir. Let's clean it up, Clifford."

I watched without a word as they meticulously put everything back in its place. They actually did make a nice, clean job of it. I emptied the chambers of both guns and tossed them their way. The older guy said, "Thank you, Mr. Copp. Sorry for the trouble. It won't happen again."

I followed them outside and watched their departure. They actually waved genially in my direction as they drove away. I went back inside, had a glass of milk, and got ready for my appointment with Chief Terry. The telephone encounter with Harley Sanford allowed me to size him up as a formidable guy. This was going to be a very interesting meeting with my in-laws. This could get brutal, maybe even nasty, but there was no way to avoid it.

THE CHIEF WAS waiting for me when I returned to the station. He was in his car and ready to roll. I climbed in beside him and said, "Hope I didn't screw anything up. I just had a brief talk with Sanford."

He was peeling out of the parking lot before he responded to that. "So how did that go?"

I replied, "I'm not sure. This guy is no dummy. I went back to the condo after I left here. I surprised Sammy and Clifford rifling Martha's apartment. I checked it out with Sanford and he seemed to confirm that he had sent them there. We didn't talk a lot, just enough for me to realize that he's tough and he's smooth. So I don't know what we are going to encounter when we get over there."

He said thoughtfully, "That's interesting. You had the impression that these goons are working for Sanford?"

"Sure, he identified them as loyal employees. What do you think of that?"

There was a long silence as the Chief threaded the police car through the midday traffic. "Bears do shit in the woods, I guess. This is interesting as hell. I have had these guys pegged as the ones responsible for the gallery fire. Yeah, very interesting."

I said, "Seems that way, yeah. How do you think he's

going to take it when he hears about his daughter's death?"

"Knowing Sanford, he'll probably hold you personally responsible, especially if he has any feeling of guilt over his relationship with her. As you know, guilty men with power don't care who they hurt. Walk with care around this guy, Joe. He's self-made and tough as a cob."

I said, "Yeah, thanks, I got that. I don't want to brawl with this guy. My heart goes out to him. But I'm not going to roll over for him either. So, what did you get from L.A.?"

Terry gave me a little embarrassed smile and replied, "Well, I hope you didn't expect me to conceal anything from these people. They know you're in town. They're very interested in that. They were also very pleased to get a positive I.D. on Martha. Of course, that is still tentative pending an official family verification. We'll have to work that with the family unless you'd rather do it yourself. Are you up to that?"

I said, "I'm not even sure I could do it. I'm still too fucked up. It's coming in bits and pieces, but it's like trying to read an image in a shattered mirror."

Chief Terry said, "Let me handle it, then. You'll like Mrs. Sanford. Don't worry about that part. If you loved Martha, you'll see a lot to love in this one, too."

We didn't say much during the rest of the drive to the Sanford estate, a palatial modern mansion with all of the amenities associated with great wealth—tennis courts, a large dome-enclosed swimming pool, Greek statuary, and acres of manicured grounds. It reeked of money. Maybe I was walking into a gigantic buzz saw. So what else was new?

# CHAPTER SIX

**C**HIEF TERRY MENTIONED that he had called ahead, and Sanford intercepted us in the driveway before we could even get out of the car. The set of the jaw told it all—he was expecting bad news. Sanford growled at Terry, "What's this all about?" He was looking bullets at me and obviously searching for my number. He shot me a harsh look and asked, "Is this *the* Joe Copp?"

I deferred to the Chief, saying simply, "Tell him."

"Tell him what?" Sanford blustered.

The Chief replied, "Let's go inside, Harley. Is Janice home?"

"She's home, dammit." He was waving us into the house. "Is it about Martha...is something wrong?"

This is always a tough job. The Chief was trying to lead him into it gently, but there is no easy way to broach this kind of news. I had been there many times myself. Sometimes the kindest way is the simple, direct truth. I told him, "We have bad news, Mr. Sanford. I think you had better get your wife."

The guy looked scared and suddenly entirely vulnerable. This was not a face he was comfortable with. He said softly, "I'll get Janice. Go on into the study."

It was a graceful home built for comfort more than

50

ostentatious display. I spotted several authentic Remingtons in the hallway, but this seemed to be the extent of his collection in contrast to the art I had seen in Martha's apartment. Unlike Martha, evidently the Sanfords preferred Western art. The study was lined with leatherbound books and I noticed a valuable Jack London collection protected behind glass.

Sanford was a man of about fifty, steel gray hair worn rather closely cropped, not exactly paunchy but beginning to soften up a bit, a shade under six feet and carrying maybe two hundred pounds. The cagey eyes had seen it all and done it all, no guy to simply roll over for any man. In contrast, Janice Sanford had evidently built a life around rolling over for this guy. Some women easily fall into that role under domineering men; I saw control written all over Harley Sanford. He ruled here. It was his domain; she was along simply for the ride.

She came into the room behind her husband, a subdued little doe of a woman—still quite pretty. I could see an occasional trace of the daughter in her appearance but none of Martha's fire. This woman had been thoroughly dominated by her husband. If she'd ever had a sense of self, it was obvious that she had lost that connection long ago.

Sanford barked at the Chief, "Let's get to it. What's happened to Martha?"

The Chief was directing his attention to both of them as he said, "This is Joe Copp. He's a private detective from Southern California. He has something to say to you about Martha."

I had the full attention of the room. Harley was devouring me with his eyes. Mrs. Sanford showed me a tense smile. I had to simply spring it. It was too brutal any other way. I told them, "Martha was killed in Los Angeles a week ago. I'm sorry it has taken so long to notify you."

Janice Sanford sagged noticeably but that was her only immediate response. Harley was stunned and made no pretense of masking it. He said, almost moaning, "Wait, something's wrong here! You don't mean that *Martha* is dead!"

I replied, "Yes, Martha is dead. She was shot to death in Los Angeles."

Sanford gave Terry an angry look and cried, "Who is this jerk? Where does he get off with this kind of crap? What is the goddamn scam here? You'll have to account for this, *Mister!*" The distraught man made a lunge at me, but the Chief intercepted his charge and softly turned him back onto his chair.

Janice stifled a little moan and gasped, "Would anyone like some coffee?" She bolted from the room before we responded.

The Chief said, "I have verified that a woman identified as Martha Kaufman was shot and killed near Los Angeles. Someone needs to identify the body. I could fly down there with you, Harley, if you'd like that. Do you think Janice is okay?"

Harley growled, "She probably didn't hear a word you said. She's just worried about being the gracious hostess. Jesus Christ! I don't believe this." He looked at me and asked, "What's your interest in all this?"

I told him, "Martha and I were married two weeks ago, Mr. Sanford. I don't know how to explain what happened because I was wounded too, and I'm having a bit of a memory problem at the moment. I don't know who shot her and I don't know why she was shot. Bet on it, though, I'm going to know. I don't expect you to think of me as a member of your family, but I would like to have at least friendly relations with you."

Sanford snarled, "I bet you would, wouldn't you! Do you have some paper on this alleged marriage?"

I produced the Nevada marriage license and gave it to the Chief. He glanced at it and passed it quickly to the distraught father. Sanford studied the document carefully, then tossed it back. He said quietly, "It's Martha's signature. Why haven't I heard about this?"

I told him, "I didn't know about it myself until a few hours ago. I'm sorry, Harley. I know this is no consolation to you, but I have hardly even known my own name since the shooting. I came to Mammoth this morning to try to put the pieces together inside my head. I am still a bit rummy, but I know that you and Janice are in a lot of pain over this and I am trying to be as honest as my memory will allow."

Sanford gave me a long hard look, then got up quickly and hurried from the room. The Chief looked at me and said, "Jesus! I told you this was going to be tough."

I replied, "Those poor people. There are never the right words for a thing like this."

Just as it seemed that we had done all that could be done here, Janice came back in with a coffee tray. The Chief helped her with it and said, "Thanks, Janice. Are you okay?"

She replied, "I'll never be okay again, but that doesn't matter anymore. Harley is the one who is probably falling apart. It was good of you men to come here at such a terrible moment. Please excuse Harley. He was devoted to Martha." She touched my hand and said gently, "You poor dear. This must be rough for you."

This was graciousness in the face of shock, and I was touched by her acceptance of me and our mutual pain. Janice Sanford was a deceptively strong woman and she was probably the one who had been holding Harley up through all the trials of their years together, and all the while he had thought the strength was his. Self-made men often have this illusion about themselves, and they frequently refuse to recognize the female qualities that hold their whole world together.

Sanford did not return that afternoon. Janice unnecessarily apologized for him. I understood something of what he must have been going through. Janice served the coffee and we sipped it in silence, waiting for Harley to reappear, but I guess she knew her husband well enough to finally say to us, "I'm sorry, Harley is probably not coming back. Chief, I will go with you to Los Angeles. We can take the company plane. How soon could you be ready to leave?"

He replied, "I could be ready within an hour unless you'd rather wait until tomorrow."

She said, "Oh, no. Let's get this over with. An hour would be fine. I'll meet you at the airport."

Terry said, "Fine," and shot me a questioning look. "Sure you wouldn't want to join us?"

I replied, "I've been there once, I couldn't do it again." I gave the lady a restrained smile and told her, "Please don't think that I don't care."

She brushed my hand with hers, and said, "I do understand."

She was a quality lady and I would have been proud to have had her as a mother-in-law. The father-in-law was still a question mark in my mind. I still didn't like the guy, but of course this could have been a premature and unfair assessment of the man. Time would tell.

WE WERE ONLY about two minutes clear of the Sanford estate when the Chief's mobile radio came alive with an urgent message. "Trouble, Chief, there's been a shooting right next door to the P.D.—an officer is down. How far away are you?"

We were cranking, even before he had his hand on the mike button. His response was, "I'm less than five minutes out, proceeding with all due speed."

The dispatcher added, "God, Chief, I only got a glimpse, but it looked just like Harley Sanford's Lincoln. This looks bad. Maybe he's heading your way. Be careful."

The Chief radioed back a tense, "Ten-four," and he punched it. We would be there in less than five minutes, for damn sure.

There seemed to be a virtual crime wave in this placid town.

I asked the Chief, "Did you hear his car leave the house?"

He replied, "I didn't hear it, no. That doesn't mean anything. With all the racket from the gardener's equipment I wouldn't have heard a Sherman tank going through there."

Now was no time for distractions. The wail of the siren and the screech of the tires hugging the winding

mountain road preempted any desire for casual conversation. This guy was rolling it. I sure didn't want to get
in his way.


THE PARAMEDICS HAD already transported the victim,
Officer Arthur Douglas, to the hospital when we hit the
scene. We had to work our way through a still-gathering
crowd to gain access. Douglas had been shot inside his
patrol car immediately after leaving the P.D. The vehicle
had rolled out of the parking lot onto the street when
the assailant apparently opened fire at close range. The
officer had been hit through the windshield and the car
had swerved across both traffic lanes and had come back
to rest against the curb almost directly in front of the
P.D. According to witnesses, Douglas had not attempted
to return fire and the consensus seemed to be that he
was shot with no apparent warning. Two other officers
were on the scene when we arrived. The Chief hurried
on over to the hospital, a few short blocks away.

I stayed behind to help with the questioning of witnesses. The shooting had occurred in full view of a line
of traffic but no one seemed to be able to offer any coherent explanation of the event. One man who claimed
to have been almost hit himself by gunfire kept repeat-
ing over and over that "the shots came from nowhere."
He added that a dozen or so cars were directly in the
traffic lanes and that it was almost a miracle that no
one else had been injured.

An incident such as this one often leaves the witnesses in a state of confusion as to the actual facts. There
seemed to be an almost unanimous agreement, however,

that the shooting had erupted from a fast-moving silver Lincoln Continental and that the gunman's vehicle sped away before the witnesses realized what had happened.

Nobody knew it yet, but a lot of trouble was headed for "River City."

# CHAPTER SEVEN

In moments such as this, time seems to stand still, even for a seasoned cop. Probably no more than five minutes had elapsed since we had hit the scene. I did what I could to assist the investigation, but the Chief's people were obviously on top of the situation so I skipped across to the P.D. for a possible lock on Harley Sanford's whereabouts. His telephone rang repeatedly without response. I gave it up after two tries.

So much for that.

I was hoping that the man could be easily accounted for during the time of the shooting in town.

Just for the hell of it, I tried Martha's number.

Bingo.

Sanford picked up on the first ring though I had to wonder for a moment if it was him. He was in a highly emotional state, maybe even crying, as he said, "Martha's not here. Oh shit—she'll never be here. God damn it, who is this?—what do you want?"

"This is Copp, Harley. Get a hold of yourself, man. How long have you been there?"

The guy was almost incoherent. I'm not sure what he said, made no sense to me, something about, "Last time around . . . "

I said, "Stay right there!"

I had left my van on the back lot of the Police Department. I told the dispatcher that I was going out to Martha's and requested that the Chief meet me there as soon as possible.

I was there in less than three minutes. I did not see his car but I went inside for a quick look, came up empty, so buzzed around the neighborhood a couple of times hoping to pick him up. There was no sign of his car so I drove on back to the condo.

The place looked exactly as I had left it that morning, nothing disturbed, no notes or anything else to give me a clue to the man's state of mind. So I called in from the condo and hurried on back to the P.D.

I got there about the same time as the Chief returned from the hospital. He was standing in the roadway as the damaged police car was being hoisted onto a tow truck. He saw me coming in and met me alongside the road.

I asked him, "How's your man?"

"He's in surgery. Looks bad. Where've you been?"

I said, "I talked to Harley on the phone. Found him at Martha's place. He sounded pretty badly screwed up. He was gone when I got there. Does this situation make any sense to you?"

This man never appeared ruffled. He seemed to be thinking about how to respond to my question. After a moment he said, "Only if Santa Claus molests little girls. I don't figure it, Joe. Why would Harley Sanford come gunning for one of my officers? We both saw the state he was in a little while ago, but he didn't seem irrational."

I said, "Well, people do strange things under stress. Any personal connection between your man and the Sanford family?"

"Yeah. He was seeing Martha not long ago. Don't know how serious it ever got, but they were definitely dating each other."

"Okay, I would call that a connection." I reflected for a moment, then said, "Seems strange that Sanford would do something like this just moments after he learns of his daughter's death."

The Chief said, "I have been wondering about that myself, but let's not jump to any quick conclusion here. You said you talked to Harley; what led you to look for him at Martha's?"

I replied, "I tried his house and got no answer. It was just a wild shot to try the condo. Figured we needed a quick fix on Sanford's Lincoln. Witnesses identified a similar car. I wanted to determine if Sanford could have been in the area at the time. I found him at the condo, which is only minutes from here. So that definitely puts him in the game. But it's your town, your game—so what do you say?"

Terry replied with an unhappy sigh. "Sounds like maybe you've got it nailed, Joe, but I still suggest caution here. Look, if Harley did it, then I want his ass, no two ways about it. But I want to be damn sure of the facts before I start busting a guy like Harley Sanford."

I told him, "Listen, the guy wasn't even coherent when I was talking with him. Now he's running around out here somewhere, apparently armed and undoubtedly dangerous. I don't think you would want to take a chance with this guy in his present state of mind."

The Chief snapped, "You're right, it *is* my town—and it's my job to call the shots here."

I said, "Hey, I wouldn't expect it any other way. Just want you to know that I'm at your disposal here. Keep in mind, though, that I also have a personal interest."

"Yeah, that's what I keep reminding myself. You're not in the clear yet yourself, bud. Don't forget it."

I told him, "Couldn't forget it. Just don't ask me to bow out. I'm probably in deep shit at home and I have to get a handle on the problem. So don't expect me to just sit around doing nothing. I'm getting a strong feeling that my problems at home are somehow intimately related to the events here in Mammoth. So use me, dammit."

The Chief gave me one of those sudden smiles as he replied, "Sorry, Joe, I shouldn't have jumped at you like that. Look, I was Faxed a hefty file on you from L.A. after our first meeting this morning. I don't have any serious reservations about you but I am also a cautious man and I don't necessarily believe everything I read. For what it's worth, I like you and I respect the way you've always handled yourself as a cop. After learning more about you, I'd have to say I can't figure you for anything dirty. But, as I said, I am a cautious man. So don't take it personal when I lean on you a little."

I told him, "Lean on me all you want, pal. While we're being so candid, let me say that you are as sharp a cop as I have ever known and I respect you, too. I can't say that about every cop I've known."

The Chief replied, "Neither can I."

A young woman whom I recognized as a police dispatcher ran from the building and called to the Chief.

"A shuttle driver just reported a vehicle over the side off Minaret Road near the ski lodge. Looks like a silver Continental. No further info at the moment."

For such a laid-back guy, the Chief can move fast when the need is there. He was halfway into his police car when he yelled at me, "Coming?"

I called back, "I'll follow you."

Which was an act of faith on my part because I knew I was in for a hell of a run with this guy. I jumped into my van and put the pedal down directly behind him. We were moving at a rather sedate pace along the heavy traffic of Main Street, but he opened it up as we hit the outskirts of town and started the five-mile climb toward Mammoth Mountain. It's a good thing I was following close because I didn't know the area that well and I had only the haziest idea of our final destination.

We were climbing steadily along a winding road west of town. The official elevation of the city itself is 8,931 feet. Mammoth Mountain, with quick and easy access from the town proper, soars to over 11,000 feet and is considered among the finest ski runs in the country. I've heard it said that skiing down the main run at Mammoth Mountain is equal to sliding down your kitchen wall. The ski lodge sits at the base of Mammoth Mountain and I believed that was about where we were headed. Though the skiers were absent this time of year, the area could be buzzing with tourists awaiting a ride on the gondola for an eagle's eye view from the top of the mountain.

The silver Lincoln was almost invisible, perched upside down in a forested area at about the 9,000-foot level and maybe a hundred yards off the road. It took a good eye to spot it.

We left our cars along the side of the road and closed quickly on the wreckage by foot. It was a silver Lincoln, okay.

But Harley Sanford was nowhere around.

A dead woman was.

I knew this victim, oh yes. I had been with her just a few short hours earlier. She was wearing a uniform suit with her name and title stitched onto the breast pocket.

I had known her only as "Cindy."

She had been shot twice in the head with a heavy-caliber weapon.

She was still warm.

I was not. This was strongly reminiscent of the scene at the L.A. County Morgue.

I was suddenly cold as ice.

And I knew that I would not be warm again until I had come face-to-face with a stone-cold killer.

I DID NOT feel that Sanford had been in the car when it took the plunge off the road. It seemed more likely that he had engaged the cruise control and jumped clear before the car had a chance to gain speed, hoping that it would bury itself in the concealing forest. All the signs I could read indicated that the pilotless vehicle had left the road at a moderate rate of speed and took a fortuitous leap toward open country, then headed into a shallow ravine where it tipped over and came to rest much closer to the road than I'm sure he had planned.

That was lucky for us because otherwise the car could have sat awhile in deep concealment before being discovered.

Between you and me and the lamppost, this did not seem to be the action of an irrational man. It could have been sheer impulse, sure, but it was certainly calculated and it could have worked.

There was certainly no joy in "Mudville" this day. It seemed that I was now to be required to investigate a slaying by my own father-in-law. I wasn't buying it yet, not all of it, but at least I would have to go through the motions—and then, pal, there was still that lovely mother-in-law to be considered.

No joy?

It was damn near insanity.

# CHAPTER EIGHT

I GUESS I was not the only one in shock here on the dark side of paradise. The Chief seemed to be no better off than I had been lately as he called in the report of this latest shooting. The poor guy appeared to be in a time warp of his own. Murder in the big city is now almost a daily event, standard routine. Violent death in a small town like this is never routine. It just is not supposed to happen here. Most of the police work in a town like Mammoth involves minor offenses and it's a real shocker when crimes of this magnitude shatter the normal tranquility.

An apparent crime spree by one of the area's leading citizens was not only unthinkable but almost unbelievable. It was no wonder that the chief of a small-town police department was beginning to feel almost overwhelmed by the crimes that had suddenly enveloped him.

Chief Terry identified the latest victim as Cindy Morgan. She was older than I had thought, but not much. Her I.D. showed her as twenty-nine, apparently single, and—according to the Chief—she had been living in the area for only about five years. There are few secrets in a small town like this, and very little goes unnoticed, especially by a sharp cop like this one. The girl had been working for the hotel since its opening two years earlier and previously had worked as a hostess at one of the finer restaurants in town.

While waiting for the coroner to arrive, the Chief cranked up his cellular telephone and tried to catch Janice Sanford at the airstrip. He was told that Mrs. Sanford was not there and had not been in touch with her pilot; the people at the airport knew nothing about any plans for a flight by the Sanford company plane, which was still in the hangar and apparently was not being prepared for flight. There was no response to insistent rings at the Sanford home.

The Chief growled, "Wonder what the hell is going on over there."

It had been just about exactly an hour since we left the Sanford home. The plan had been that the Chief would meet Mrs. Sanford at the airport an hour later for the flight to Los Angeles. She would have called the pilot immediately to get the plane serviced and ready to fly.

Something was wrong out there.

I told the Chief, "This sounds bad. I tried to call Harley at home before connecting with him at the condo, which was just a few minutes after we hit town, and there was no answer at that time. Janice seemed to be reliable and anxious to identify her daughter's body. I can't believe that she would simply change her mind about that and not notify you of the change of plans."

The Chief replied, "I'm with you on that. I'm worried. I'll have to take a run out to their place as soon as we finish up here."

I said, "Well, I told you to use me. Would you like it if I went?"

The Chief gave me an uneasy look and replied, "Yes, thanks, I'd feel better if I knew that Janice was okay. Christ, Joe, it has been a nutty day. To tell you the truth, I am very worried about Janice. As for Harley, he has always been a stand-up guy for my money. I am not willing to condemn the man until I know all the facts. There is no solid evidence that Harley is responsible for these shootings. Okay...maybe he was...and maybe he wasn't. I just don't want to fry him on conjecture, I'd like to know what it's all about. But God damn it, Joe, how would a man like Harley Sanford get himself into this kind of mess? I can't buy it unless the man has totally flipped his wig. I did not get that sensing from Harley when we were over there."

I told him, "This sort of thing is never easy to figure, Chief, but I guess it could happen to anybody when the circumstances take you over the edge. Was he in any financial difficulties?"

"Hell, I don't know. I guess maybe sometimes the bigger they are, the harder they fall, but if Harley was in that kind of trouble I never heard anything about it. This guy started with nothing. If he has ended up with nothing, at this point in his life, maybe it could take him over the edge. He's a proud man, I know that, but he would be more the type to blow his own brains out in a situation like that, not somebody else's."

I said, "Well, you know the man better than I do. Just don't bet your life on it."

I slid out of the seat and showed him a sympathetic smile as I hurried on to my van. He watched me leave but did not return my wave as I turned across the road and headed back toward town. Poor guy was in a hell of a state over this, but that just showed the man's heart, not any weakness.

I ran on back to the Sanford place, took only about ten minutes. Took me almost that long to find someone on the premises. A young man, whom I'd seen gardening earlier, finally showed himself outside a garage at the rear and came over to greet me. I asked him, "Nobody home?"

This kid was a wiseass. He said, "I'm home. What can I do for you?"

Somehow you can spot these guys, the type who come on tough but fold up at the sight of a badge. I had his number. He took a too-quick look at my P.I. badge and changed his tone instantly before even realizing that I was a private cop. He asked me, "What's the problem, officer?"

I reminded him, "We saw each other earlier today. Where are the Sanfords?"

He told me, "They went out. Is something wrong?"

I said, "Could be. I was supposed to meet Mrs. Sanford at the airport. She didn't get there. What do you know about that?"

The guy replied, "Uh ... she tore out of here about ... I wasn't watching the time but it was right after you left here a while ago."

I asked him, "Did you notice when Mr. Sanford left?"

"Just before you left," he said.

"Was he driving his Lincoln?"

"Yes, sir. Mrs. Sanford drove her BMW."

"Any idea where Mrs. Sanford was headed?"

"No, sir. They don't usually keep me posted on their activities."

I gave the guy a knowing smile and thanked him. Next stop was the hotel where Cindy Morgan had worked.

An older woman was at the front desk. She was about fifty, friendly—almost too friendly—but I did not remember seeing her before. I asked her, "What time did Cindy go off duty?"

The woman replied, "She works a split shift on weekdays." She gave me an almost flirting smile. "She's due back at six. Could I help you with something?"

I told her, "Maybe you could. Do you know Harley Sanford?"

"Sure, I know Mr. Sanford," she replied.

"Do you see him often?"

She gave me another teasing smile. "Not nearly as often as Cindy sees him."

"What does that mean?"

She covered it with a laugh and said, "I was just kidding."

I said, "Of course you weren't," and gave her a wink.

She gave me a wink in response as she said, "People do talk. Weren't you staying here a few weeks ago?"

I said, "Yeah, I'm Joe Copp. I'm a police investigator and I've been doing some work with the local police department."

That information intrigued her. Didn't seem necessary to explain that I was a *private* investigator. I checked her name tag as I leaned close to show her a confidential wink. "Did you see Cindy leave here with Sanford a little while ago, Marie?"

She replied in almost a stage whisper, "Yes. Oh, well,

I'm not sure about today. I didn't actually see the car, but he's been picking her up here just about every day for months. For lunch, of course, or so they say. Look, I'm not just gossiping, everybody in town knows what's going on. That is, maybe everyone except his daughter. She and Cindy are close friends, so I can't imagine that she would know about it. You know these small towns, they're practically soap operas—everybody is connected with everybody else, and they all know each other's business."

"You're speaking of Martha Kaufman, right?"

"Yes. She owned the art gallery that burned recently."

"Have you heard about the policeman who was shot today?"

She replied, "Did I *hear!* I was about a block away. It sounded like the Fourth of July. Poor man, I hope he's going to be okay. What was *that* all about? I can hardly believe that a thing like that has happened here. It really shakes you up."

I said, "Yeah, it sure does. Afraid we don't have any answers yet. We're still trying to sort it out. Uh . . . listen, Marie . . . you seem to have most of the scoop around here; do you think that Janice Sanford knows about her husband's 'lunches' with Cindy?"

"That poor woman, how could she not know? God, it's been one after another for years. For all I know, maybe he goes home and boasts about his indiscretions. Certainly he has never seemed interested in trying to conceal it."

I said, " 'Peyton Place,' huh?"

" 'Peyton Place' was before my time," she said teasingly.

I teased her back—"Sure, sorry. Mine too. Guess I was thinking of 'Dallas.'"

She was having fun with it. "You don't look like a soap-opera man, Joe. I'm sure you can find more interesting ways to spend your nights. But if you need any suggestions..."

"God, Marie, you'll have the whole town talking about us."

She said laughingly, "I don't care if you don't."

I told her, "Sure, you say that now, but how will it feel when the entire police department is talking about you?"

"I could handle it," she replied soberly.

I kissed her on the lips and beat it out of there. I was not sure that I could handle it. Especially not in this town. Paradise? Not really. There was no such place in the world I knew. Didn't seem to matter the size or the name, the whole world seemed to be intent upon devouring itself despite all the efforts of the finest and the sweetest among us. If that sounds like a cynical cop, then let me wear that label for a minute—it comes to all of us at one time or another, and this seemed to be my turn.

A dark thought suddenly struck me.

Had Mrs. Sanford noticed her husband's absence after the chief and I departed, and went searching for him? Had she found him?

God, I hoped not.

This thing had become twisted enough without adding further complicating factors.

But what could have sent Harley Sanford gunning murderously for two people? What set him off? Was it simply grief that sent him over the edge? Was it revenge? Or could it have been an overpowering guilt?

I almost did not want to know the answer to that. Even less did I desire to know the truth about Janice Sanford's possible leap into the darkness. I liked that woman. Already she'd had enough heartache.

Something dark and scary was whispering at me. Something almost already known or at least suspected, and maybe too terrible to contemplate. If so, could I handle that truth, or had it been blotted from my mind as a merciful amnesia to shelter a knowledge too terrible to face?

What kind of guilt, what fearful truth could I be hiding from even my own mind?

Had I crossed the threshold into every good cop's worst nightmare?

And what have I been trying to hide, even from myself?

*My God, what could I be guilty of here on this darkest side of paradise?*

# CHAPTER NINE

CHIEF TERRY HAD returned to the police department only moments ahead of me. The Morgan girl's body had been transported to the county morgue and Terry was in a foul mood. That is understandable; it's a rotten task under the best of circumstances, the very worst in a small town like this where no death is impersonal—where, indeed, every death is intensely personal. A homicide is particularly ugly and shattering because it touches the darkest fear of the human heart. It is the personification of evil and confusion when it strikes this close to home.

The Chief crankily told me, "I could have saved you a trip. There was a message from Janice waiting for me when I got back. She decided to drive into L.A., said she needed some time to settle her mind anyway. I'm not surprised. She always had a fear of flying, especially in these smaller private jobs. What did you pick up out there?"

I replied, "Not a hell of a lot. One of the workers told me that Sanford took off while we were still there—which we already knew, of course—and that Janice had left just after us, which I guess also is old information now. So, what is your sensing on all this?"

The Chief replied, "Why don't you ask me something simple? I put out an APB on Harley while I was waiting for the coroner. So there is a periodic surveillance on his other homes. I don't expect him to show up there, but at least we're covering the bases. Does that meet with your approval?"

I said, "Fuck it. Since when have you sought my approval?"

The guy chuckled at me and said, "Fuck you, too."

I chuckled with him. We were both drawing blanks and we knew it. Poor bastard, I couldn't blame him. His town was caving in around him; two more homicides and he'd be out of a job. I asked him, "How much longer 'til your retirement?"

The Chief said, "Retirement, hell. Two more homicides and I'll be out of a job."

I told him, "You just read my mind, pal."

He said, "If I was a drinking man, I'd have a snort right now. Maybe I'll have one anyway."

I said, "Maybe we could classify it as justifiable therapy."

He uncorked a "short dog" of Jack Daniels from his file drawer and said, "Justifiable or not, fuck it. Let's do it."

It was a very short bottle, maybe one good snort for each of us. Drinking man or not, this guy punched it in a single gulp. I did the same and immediately regretted it. We both grimaced appropriately and shivered with the expanding burn from the Tennessee sour mash.

I've been for hire, been on fire, been in deep and in the dark, even been on ice, and for days I'd been in shock, but that snort capped it all and released the tensions that had put us both on edge. We had become pals again. Whatever your feelings about "the devil's brew," and all its reputed evils, both of us needed that. We would find later that we were going to need much more than that bottle had to offer us.

I WENT WITH the Chief to look in on Arthur Douglas, the officer who had been shot earlier. The hospital waiting room was loaded with family and friends anxiously awaiting further word on the officer's condition. They all came to instant attention as we arrived, as though Chief Terry's presence would make it better. A woman of about fifty with wet eyes rose quickly to greet the Chief. He hugged her warmly, gently patted her on the back, and said, "God, I'm sorry, Jean. Have you heard anything?"

She told him, "They just brought Art back from surgery. The doctor thinks he's going to be okay, but his condition is guarded. They let me in to see him for a couple of minutes, but he hasn't come around yet. Who could have done this, John?"

The Chief replied, "Don't worry, we're working on that." He motioned me over and introduced me. "This is Joe Copp, he's been working with me on this. Joe is a special investigator from Los Angeles, an old hand at this sort of thing."

A youth of about twenty with an insincere handshake, maybe a bit still wet behind the ears, rudely asked me, "What does L.A. have to do with this?"

I told him, "Maybe nothing. I just happened to be in the area investigating another matter. What do you think happened?"

The kid looked sharp. It turned out he was a cousin of the wounded officer. He said, "Seems obvious to me what happened. From what I heard, Art was shot by that big-deal developer, Harley Sanford. What more do you need to know? That bastard isn't going to get away with this, is he?"

I said, "I wish it were that easy, but things are often not what they seem to be. The Chief is on top of it. You've got a..."

The kid jumped right up my frame, and maybe he had a right to. He snorted, "Aw, bullshit. You guys all say that but nothing ever really gets changed. If that guy gets away with this..."

Jean Douglas hurried into that breach and shushed her nephew with a soft reprimand. She told him, "The police are doing all they can."

This chief was able to speak for himself. He told the kid, "Sit down and behave yourself, Danny. This isn't the time for this."

Nothing is more disheartening than distraught loved ones demanding justice before the facts are in. But the kid had something. With Officer Douglas unable to contribute to the investigation and with Cindy Morgan silenced forever, we were back to square one.

Justice is not always a quick fix. As frustrating as it may sometimes be, frontier justice is a thing of the past. Modern police work is an endless round of legalities and technicalities, which often seem to do as much to frustrate justice as to serve it. Every cop recognizes the limitations of the system and any good cop knows that he has to operate within those limitations. I could sympathize with the families of victims such as Arthur Douglas. It all seems so cold and impersonal to the layman who is not familiar with all the nuances of the criminal justice system. It is frustrating for all of us, sure, and especially for the average cop who is charged with the preservation of our civilization. None of us who care want the cop to be above the law. But we should understand that he is working for all of us, in an uncertain and hazardous arena. As the last line between civilization and savagery, our cops must be supported. The alternative is chaos.

I went into the intensive care unit with the Chief. Douglas was heavily sedated and we both knew that there was nothing we could learn from him at this time, but it was more than a perfunctory call as neither of us had found the opportunity to examine the physical evidence.

This guy looked like death. He had been hit in both shoulders and took another slug in the upper chest, narrowly missing the heart. The surgeons must have had a hell of a time with this one. Tubes and hoses were strung all over the guy and several machines quietly monitored his tenuous hold on life. I was pleased to find that the chief had seen fit to order preservation of all of the physical evidence that had accompanied the officer in the ambulance. All of it had been professionally bagged and cataloged and was waiting for us in a corner of the room.

It would not seem logical that the man had been shot out of the blue for no reason. Drive-by shootings may be commonplace in my neck of the woods but I doubt that things could have gotten that bad in this small mountain community. And drive-by shootings are rarely, if ever, committed anywhere by respected citizens.

None of the eyewitnesses had actually identified Harley Sanford as the shooter—there was only a tentative I.D. of the car itself.

So...it followed that this daring attempted murder in broad daylight, directly outside the police station, in full view of numerous witnesses, was either an irrational random act or a calculated attack by a desperate man with everything to win and nothing to lose. I had to read it that way. So if Sanford had been the shooter, then what had driven him to risk it all? Had he really rolled the dice for keeps?

We went into the nurses' lounge and found a quiet place to go through the evidence. The Chief opened the bag and together we examined Officer Douglas's belongings. The contents revealed a man of precise organization who carefully arranged his working routines. Among other things we found were an expensive watch, a wallet with several credit cards and a little bit of cash, a police academy ring, address book, a pack of cigarettes neatly drilled dead center by a bullet, a lighter, a bloody shirt punctured by three bullets, two large-caliber, distorted slugs—one of the slugs was never recovered. It was notable that his gun had not been fired.

This was routine stuff except for the final item in the pocket of his bloodstained shirt. It was a note passed to Douglas by the police dispatcher, time-stamped at 12:45 P.M. the day of the shooting: *Art—I'm worried. It's ur-*

*gent that you meet me at the Chart House as soon as you start your shift. Cindy Morgan.*

I told the Chief, "This could be pay dirt. Why do you think she sent an urgent message to one of your officers? How well did she know this guy?"

He said, "Hell, this is a small town, Joe. She's been living in Mammoth for at least five years and she has worked all over town. Christ, I don't know if they had anything going. Cops do get around..."

I said, "And so did Cindy. Do you know that she was seeing Sanford on a regular basis?"

He replied, "Yeah, everybody in town was whispering about them."

I asked, "Do you think Mrs. Sanford knew about it?"

"Well, she's no dummy."

"So what do you think we had going here? Looks to me like a lot of inner connections."

I was going through Douglas's address book. He was one of these guys who flags significant phone numbers. There was a flag on Janice Sanford, one on Cindy Morgan, and a double on Martha Kaufman, with both home and gallery emphasized.

But the biggest jolt of all... *Douglas had flagged my home address and telephone number in Los Angeles!*

What the hell?

Something ominous was rumbling through my head, an expanding realization that I was embroiled in a web of intrigue and murder, extending from the Eastern Sierra halfway across the state to the metropolis of Los Angeles.

The only connection I knew for sure was my marriage

to Martha Kaufman—and I couldn't even remember that.

But what did I really know about any of these people?

Could they be connected to my own shooting in L.A?

*Was it possible that all these people had died because I had not?*

# CHAPTER TEN

I SHOWED CHIEF Terry the notation with my listing in Douglas's address book and asked him, "What do you know about this?"

The Chief gave me a puzzled look as he replied, "I don't know why he would have you in his book except that he had known Martha since they were kids. He probably knew that Martha had become involved with you, so maybe he just wanted to get your pedigree. I don't see anything sinister about that."

I said, "Yeah, but look at it, John. You've been a cop long enough to know that a series of killings does not exist in a vacuum. Shortly after Martha and I were married, somebody killed Martha and tried to kill me. I would call that a connection. To compound it, now, I have been back in town less than a day and already there have been two more shootings. I have to call that also a connection. Haven't you noticed the progression in Douglas's list? Is Janice Sanford the next victim?"

The Chief growled, "That's a hell of a stretch, isn't it? If you start suspecting everyone who knows all the victims, you have to include most of the people in my town."

I replied, "Who's talking about suspects? This is a

victim list. Douglas is a victim himself, not a suspect."

"Sure, but it's his list that is setting you off. Looks to me like you're trying to connect my officer with a string of killings."

I told him, "No, you've got your ass in this, John. It reads to me like maybe your cop was onto something. That could be why someone tried to take him out."

The Chief said, "Sorry . . . I was emoting, not thinking. You may be right there, Joe."

I said, "Yeah. Just how friendly were Douglas and Martha? You're a sensitive guy, and I appreciate that, but you've been a bit less than candid with me in regard to Martha. So stop being sensitive. What have you not told me about those two?"

The Chief gave me an embarrassed smile. "It didn't seem to be either pertinent or appropriate to talk about that. Look, Joe, Martha was a full-grown woman and certainly too young to be a widow forever. I'm sure you know that she had been dating before she met you. I was not intentionally being less than candid—I just did not see any relevance."

The Chief had buttoned up the evidence bag and we were preparing to get out of there when a disturbance outside the nurses' lounge attracted our attention. A youthful voice yelled, "Get down! Get down!"

We flew into the corridor to investigate the ruckus. Two men carrying sawed-off shotguns had invaded the waiting room and were moving swiftly toward the Intensive Care Unit. People were scattering in panic as though they had been ordered to hit the floor and were complying with all possible haste. The gunmen were professionals; there was no hesitation or confusion as they swept through the waiting area and unerringly along the hallway leading to the I.C.U.

They spotted us the moment we emerged and they were tracking down on us instantly. The Chief and I moved together almost like a team and hit the deck beneath a narrow ledge as two quick rounds exploded from both shotguns and shattered a window directly behind us. The shooters were experts and were not playing for effect. These were automatics and were limited only by the agility of the shooter. Two of them were laying down on us with murderous intent and the only thing that saved our day was the Chief's big .357 Magnum, which was bracketing them instantly with return fire. I yelled at him, "Toss me the bag!"

There were no standing targets out there. These guys were firing on the run. The Chief had already anticipated my play. He tossed me holster and all from the evidence bag and snarled, "You got it, bud!"

And just in time. I caught it on the slide and executed a perfect pirouette worthy of the Bolshoi Ballet and came up firing at the precise moment that two other deadly blasts shattered the doorway I had just vacated. After that stunt, I would recommend a twirl or two of police training with the Bolshoi; that one undoubtedly saved my life.

We were a pretty good team, each selecting his own target with calm precision and withering accuracy. The Chief cried, "These turkeys are ours, bud."

That much was obvious, and they knew it. They had already broken for a quick retreat. They did not make it. In a running firefight, the advantage is with the cooler hand. These two had made the mistake of trying to run and fight at the same time. I am proud to say that John Terry is a very cool hand under fire. His man took two big hits from the .357 that blasted him through a glass wall of the building onto the sidewalk outside. My target caught it at a dead run and was catapulted into a death slide that came to rest inside the waiting room.


THE FIRST ONE off the floor was Douglas's young cousin, Danny. He yelled, "Is everyone okay?" A sharp kid who wasn't wet behind the ears anymore. He ran toward me as I cautiously approached the fallen body of the gunman I had taken down.

I warned the kid, "Careful there, careful, let's be sure this one is out of it."

But there was no cautioning this kid. I believe he would have attacked the dead body if I had not intervened. I firmly pushed him away and confirmed that the gunman was no longer a threat. The Chief had gone through the shattered window to verify his hit. Jean Douglas and other family members rose on shaky feet and were trying to get themselves together. Several of the women were weeping while others were nervously chattering about their close call.

A number of hospital workers were beginning to come forward and take charge of their hospital again. They were running from room to room, reasserting their control, professionally reassuring and calming frightened patients. A young doctor, who may have been an intern, was checking vital signs of the assailants. I could have told him with no medical training whatever that there would be no vital signs to record here.

The Chief vaulted over the window sash and back into the room, then quickly verified the condition of my man. He snorted, "Jesus! I think I'm flashing back to Vietnam!"

I told him, "Pal, I always want you on my side. That was a sweet shoot."

He replied, "Ditto double, bud. Obviously your rep is not all hype. Were you in 'Nam?"

I said, "No, I missed that one."

The Chief said, "Too bad. I've got to go check on Douglas." He disappeared into I.C.U. and returned momentarily and assured me, "It's all okay back there."

There were a lot of shocked and frightened faces in evidence but, thank God, no one else had been hurt, and that was amazing as the place looked like a war zone. There were holes in the walls, broken window glass littered the floor, and various pieces of medical equipment lay in disarray. You're normally not counting at a time like this, but there must have been at least a dozen shots fired all together from the shotguns; I remembered watching one guy coolly reloading at some point during this. It was a daring hit in every way, comparable to any big-city assassination attempt by the Mob.

There was already a response from two police agencies. A Mono County sheriff's car swooped in from one end while a city police car screeched through from the opposite side. These guys came in with guns drawn and prepared for whatever. They both seemed a bit disappointed to discover that the action had ended without them. Chief Terry called them over and updated them on the situation. Both officers then assisted in the interviewing of witnesses while Terry and I tried to get a make on the assassins.

These guys were real pros. There were no I.D.'s on the bodies and no hint as to their origins except for a General Motors automobile key found on one of them. Terry sent an officer outside to look for their car. It was instant pay dirt. A rented Chevy Caprice with the engine running was found parked illegally in a handicapped zone directly opposite the hospital entrance. We later discovered that the car had been stolen from a rental lot in Lake Tahoe.

I told the Chief, "I don't think these guys came gunning for you or me. Obviously they came to finish the job on Douglas."

"Obviously, yeah. So solve it for me, Joe."

I replied, "Screw you, pal, it's your town and your dirty laundry. Who was gunning for me in L.A.? Who killed Martha? Who needed Cindy and Douglas silenced? Who had the money to finance all of that? You've been telling me what a stand-up guy Sanford is, so where the hell is he now and who else do you know that could afford to finance all of this?"

The Chief said, "I love your simple fucking questions, Joe."

I said, "So why don't you give me a simple fucking answer, pal. Is Sanford bankrolling all this crap?—and is it conceivable that he would even have his own daughter hit?"

"Jesus, Joe, don't lay that on me. I can't get a handle on this kind of insanity. There's no logic. Why would Harley Sanford have his own daughter murdered?"

"For that matter, why have his lover murdered in his own car in a very incriminating manner? If you're going to kill someone and hope to cover it up, you don't do it the way this guy did it. This is a nutty case, but there is a logic at work here somewhere. We need to look closer at the Arthur Douglas connection. Let's go to his place."

Terry replied, "Just let me clear up a couple of important matters. I want a brief word with the Douglas family and I need to order an around-the-clock guard on his room."

"Good idea. I'll meet you outside. Could we grab a bite to eat along the way? I haven't eaten anything really since I hit town this morning. How about The Chart House?"

The Chief said, "Christ, you think of eating at a time like this?—oh, I think I know what you have in mind. Okay, right. I'll meet you in a minute."

I was happy to have a moment outside. The Chief was right, I really wasn't in that much of a mood for food at a time like this, but the connection between Douglas and Cindy was bothering the hell out of me. Something was cooking inside my skull and I needed to let it gestate.

Also I had to admit that the hunger pangs had begun working at me, despite the carnage, and for some odd reason a shooting like this always made me hungry. Maybe it was a defense mechanism having something to do with a release of tension in a time of stress. A lot of cops I have known developed weight problems, so maybe that has something to do with it.

Also, although it may sound paradoxical, it seemed that the stress was beginning to clear my head and I was feeling more like the old Joe again.

Yeah, the old Joe again, except that it felt like I was trying to claw myself out of the ninth ring of Hell. Even so, it was preferable to the confusion I had been experiencing the last twenty-four hours.

So welcome home, sucker.

Maybe you'll even be a cop again.

# CHAPTER ELEVEN

YOU NEED TO have a bit of feeling for the topography of this little mountain community. It is not a "one-horse town." In fact, Mammoth has at least five or six "horses" and its most prominent characteristic is a diverse spread with no apparent regard for municipal planning. There seems to be no center to the business area; it's just here, there, and everywhere, a crazy-quilt pattern almost in defiance of normal zoning practices. Don't plan on scouting around this area without some transportation.

My memory of the area was returning in scattered little bits and pieces; The Chart House plopped in on me the moment we stepped inside. There is a chain of these restaurants sprinkled throughout California, each definitely upscale and popular, and each individually tailored to its own particular locale. I would suppose that there are no two exactly alike, but I knew instantly that I had been inside this one before, yes, and more than once. I did not recall the details but there was a strong déjà-vu quality to the memory.

Chief Terry was a popular man in this town. We received instant attention and easy camaraderie from the staff. Obviously word of the crime wave had spread like wildfire and we were besieged by expressions of shocked disbelief.

"I can't believe it!"

"Not in Mammoth!"

"I'm worried about my kids!"

"Who could have done something like this?"

The Chief coolly reassured one and all that the proper steps were being taken and tried to assuage their concerns. What could the poor guy say, after all?

We took a booth in a secluded area at the rear, hoping to get a moment to ourselves. Still everyone, it seemed, continued to stop by and express regret, so it took a few minutes before things settled down.

We ordered dinner and I asked the waitress if she could send the hostess over to our table. As soon as the waitress departed, the Chief asked me, "What's that all about?"

I told him, "Trying to get a line on your man Douglas, to clarify that note from Cindy Morgan."

He said, "Gotcha. Not sure where you're headed with that, but it couldn't cost anything."

I replied, "I'm hoping for a sensing on the relationship between those two. Seems like Douglas has had a lot of involvements with the young women of this town. Hell, I don't know what I'm going for, John. I'm just flaying around, hoping to find a handle."

At this moment an attractive young woman walked up to our table and said, "You asked to see me, Chief Terry?"

The Chief said, "Yes, Rachel. This is Joe Copp, an investigator from Los Angeles. He's been working with me on this. He wants to talk to you."

Rachel forced a solemn little smile as she replied, "Sure, I remember Joe. I heard about the shooting at the hospital. That's terrible. Is it true that Cindy Morgan is dead?"

He replied, "I'm afraid so."

I told her, "We feel that there must be a connection between Cindy's death and the shooting of Officer Douglas. We're just trying to make some sense of all this." I gave her a reassuring smile, hoping to put her more at ease. "Were they in here today?"

She replied, "Not them, no. Cindy was in here alone around noon."

I asked, "Do you know if she made a phone call while she was here?"

She said, "I don't know about that, but she received a call."

"When was that?"

She replied, "Ah, I think...the call was from Harley Sanford...she seemed upset. Wait a minute...she did make a call right after that. Just after her conversation with Harley...ah, yeah, I remember seeing her placing a call at the pay phone outside the ladies' lounge."

"So that would have been about...?"

"Let's see...I seated the Anderson party of six at exactly twelve forty-five...I'm sure of that...yes!...she was at the pay phone outside the lounge when I seated the Anderson party. When I returned to my station, Cindy was sitting at the bar."

I asked, "Did you see Cindy leave?"

"No, I didn't. That was our rush hour and I was really swamped."

"The last time you saw her she was sitting at the bar?"

"Yes."

I angled a glance at the Chief and said, "Maybe we need to talk to that bartender."

She said, "I'll send him back if you'd like."

I thanked her and the Chief added, "Thanks, Rachel."

The girl seemed relieved that the cross-examination was over. She went on toward the bar and the Chief told me, "The bartender is a guy named Eddie. He's okay, local boy, keeps his nose clean."

I said, "Let's hope so." My mind was hung up on something else. "I noticed that Sanford's car had a telephone. It seems obvious, doesn't it, that Sanford called Cindy right after he left us at his house?"

"Yeah, I agree. And Cindy left that message for Douglas with the dispatcher only minutes after she took the call from Sanford."

"Right. And a few minutes later we have the Douglas shooting. Would it seem reasonable that a man has a standing date with his lover and along the way, only two blocks from here, lies in wait to shoot a police officer? Does that make sense? For damn sure this was not a random shooting. Whoever the shooter was, he knew that Douglas would be coming out of that parking lot at one o'clock."

Before the Chief could respond to this, the bartender came over. He was a nice-looking guy of about thirty-five, immaculate in his bar uniform and obviously very sharp. He came to us with a genial smile and focused on the Chief as he asked, "Did you want to see me, Chief?"

Terry replied soberly, "Meet Joe Copp. He's working

with me on our problem. Joe wants a word with you, Eddie."

The bartender seemed a bit nervous, which was understandable under the circumstances. He showed us a tense smile as he replied, "Yes, I remember Mr. Copp. He's the Spanish wine expert—right?"

I told him, "I don't know about the expert part, but you do have a mean sherry here."

Eddie said, "Nobody else has ordered that lately. I still have a supply. Would you like me to bring you a bottle?"

I said, "Thanks, Eddie, not right now." Martha had been the one with the fondness for sherry. I never really liked it myself, but maybe I had acquired the taste during the time I had spent with her. It was strange the way isolated little memories would come flooding back on me and hurt like hell. I swallowed the pain and continued, "You heard about Cindy Morgan?"

He replied, "Yeah, that was terrible. I served her a drink just a few hours ago."

I asked him, "Was she in here alone?"

"Well, yeah—until Mr. Sanford dashed in and pulled her out of here."

"You mean he literally pulled her out?"

"Yes, almost literally. He wouldn't give her time to finish her drink."

"You would say that he was upset about something?"

"Oh yeah."

"Did he tell you what he was upset about?"

"Not to me, no, but he told Cindy that someone had nearly killed him."

"Did he explain that?"

"Not that I heard. There was some back-and-forth between them but I didn't hear it all. I figured he meant that someone had tried to cut him off the road or something."

"So then what happened?"

"Nothing happened. He tossed some money at me and they were gone before I could even make his change."

"But let's get this straight—Sanford claimed that somebody had tried to kill him?—is that the way he said it?"

"Yes, that's exactly what he said—'Someone nearly killed me.'"

I said, "And he didn't say that calmly."

"No sir, that's right. I told you he was in a sweat."

"You didn't tell me that, Eddie."

"Sorry. But that's exactly the way it sounded, he was in a sweat, and he couldn't get out of here fast enough."

I said, "Thanks, Eddie, that's helpful. What can you tell me about Cindy's frame of mind before Sanford arrived?"

"She seemed worried, maybe a bit agitated. Look, working in a bar you get a slice of everyone's life, the good and the bad. She had her problems like all of us have."

I said, "Do you know anything about the relationship between Cindy and Douglas?"

"They knew each other, but Cindy knew a lot of guys. Douglas comes in often after work. He knows a lot of girls."

"You can talk plainer than that. This is a murder investigation."

"There were no strings on Cindy. She came and went

as she pleased. I don't know what she saw in Harley Sanford. He sure as hell wasn't paying her bills. She was very independent. I know that she was very troubled today, the last time I saw her."

"You still haven't told me about Cindy and Douglas. She called him from here earlier today. What do you think that could have been about?"

"Hell, I don't know. She didn't talk to me about it."

"Were Cindy and Douglas sleeping together?"

The guy was trying to sound honest and dumb at the same time. "Oh, that's what you were getting at. I thought I gave you that. Sure, I guess they were sleeping together now and then."

I said, "Well, we finally got that in the open."

He said, "Look, guys, I wasn't trying to be evasive. I live in this town and I work with all these people. Most of them are friends of mine. I'm just not comfortable talking intimately about my customers. You can understand that."

"Sure, I can understand that," I replied.

Eddie asked, "Is there anything else I can help you with?"

I said, "Is there anything else you'd like to tell us?"

He replied, "Not that I can think of. If something else should come to me, I'll let you know."

"Do that."

Our dinner arrived. I thanked the bartender with a friendly pat on the shoulder and he made a quick retreat.

It was a stand-up dinner. The steak was great and reminded me how little I had eaten over the past several days. We finished the meal in silence, probably both of us lost in our own introspections. Nice thing about being in the company of a guy like this one, there was no need to pad the mind with small talk.

We passed on the dessert and were working on the bill when Eddie, the bartender, returned with an air of excitement and with a proud declaration: "I just thought of something, Chief. Mr. Copp told me to let him know if I remembered anything else."

I asked, "What have you got, Eddie?"

He was beaming when he reported, "Somebody came in this afternoon not long after Mr. Sanford left. I thought you'd want to know."

The Chief was sounding a bit impatient as he said, "Let's have it, Eddie."

"It was Mrs. Sanford. She came looking for her husband. I think I told her I hadn't seen him. I mean, you know, it was a delicate situation."

I replied, "You're saying that she came into The Chart House after the shooting at the police department?"

He said, "Yes, sir, that's what I'm saying. Several customers came in after Douglas was shot and they were talking about it. That's why I'm sure of the timing."

So maybe this was putting a new slant on the story.

Why had Janice Sanford come all the way back into town looking for her husband shortly after the Chief and I had left her, when supposedly she was preparing for her flight to Los Angeles? Was it because she knew that her husband was meeting his lover at such a time? Could that have been too much for this woman to swallow, with her daughter lying dead in the county morgue?

Had she never intended to meet the Chief at the airport?—or had she been delayed by more pressing matters? Could Janice Sanford have been capable of murder?

Of course; any women could be driven to murder by a cruelly insensitive husband. Every cop knew that because every cop had seen this particular form of brutalization many times.

Evidently she had known precisely where to come looking for her husband. Had she found him? Is there a limit to what a woman could put up with, even a woman like Janice Sanford?

Did either of us actually know for sure that she had left for Los Angeles as her message to the Chief indicated—or had she still been in the Mammoth area when Cindy Morgan was killed?

I had to keep reminding myself that the Sanfords were my in-laws, and also that they were virtual strangers to me. There could be many surprising revelations about those two before this case was finished.

I had to be on the alert for anything that might come my way. The way things had been developing, there were nothing but bombshells ahead.

# CHAPTER TWELVE

ARTHUR DOUGLAS HAD a small bachelor apartment in Old Mammoth, site of the original village. Miners once panned for gold nearby. The U.S. Forest Service had been instrumental in developing Mammoth as a summer resort area during the 1920s, hoping to attract more visitors to the region. In later years the commercial development of "white gold" attracted thousands to the winter ski slopes.

We did not have a formal search warrant in hand, but Chief Terry figured we had the next best thing. A judge had okayed the entry of the officer's home and promised that the paperwork would follow.

But someone had beaten us to it.

The place had been trashed. Whatever had been the object of the search, it had been a furious one. Everything had been pulled from all the kitchen cabinets, the refrigerator had been emptied, all the contents—even milk and ice cream—had been dumped onto the floor, and a small dining table had been upended. A VCR had been overturned, racks of videotapes systematically inspected, tapes pulled from their cases and discarded in a pile. Couch cushions had been slashed.

They had not spared the bedroom either. The mattresses had been pulled off the bed and slashed, the contents of dresser drawers scattered about. Clothing had been pulled from the closet and ransacked.

These people had done a total demolition job. They had methodically gone through the apartment with a fine-toothed comb. It was not for fun and games. They obviously had been searching for something small enough to have been concealed within a milk carton or videotape case. The two who invaded Martha's condo earlier had been total gentlemen compared to the ones who did this.

The Chief said, "Bastards!"

I replied, "Evidently they knew what they were looking for."

The Chief gingerly knelt alongside the mess from the refrigerator and poked at the debris. He retrieved a small, broken, electric clock that had been torn from the wall above the kitchen stove. "Take a look at this."

The clock had stopped at 3:17.

I said, "Our friends were busy before they invaded the hospital. Any doubt that it wasn't the same two guys?"

"No, I guess not. I've never seen anyone work a place this thoroughly. What the hell could they have been looking for?"

I replied, "Maybe the same thing Sanford was looking for at Martha's apartment."

The Chief said, "That's possible. I can't believe that these are unrelated events."

I told him, "You are buying into a very sticky wicket here, pal. If we go with that thesis, then all of these problems—including the death of Martha—are linked. Are you ready to go for that?"

"Hell, I guess we're already there. It *is* all linked."

I said, "Then Martha was linked. I was linked. Everyone who has been affected by Martha's death is linked. Is that too stiff for you?"

"Not for me, no. It just seems to be the only thing that makes sense."

"Sooner or later we have to come to the obvious implications of all this. This stuff has organized crime written all over it. You've hinted at that yourself, Chief."

"Don't give me credit for an original idea. If there had been any illusions about that earlier, our 'Gunfight at the O.K. Corral' certainly locked it in. They were 'mob' okay." The Chief looked at his watch and said, "Speaking of which, I should have had a line on those guys by now."

I said, "We're not going to find anything worthwhile here." I picked up the remains of a picture frame from the living room carpet. It had suffered the same treatment that everything else in this apartment had been subjected to. The glass frame was in pieces and even the photograph itself had been torn. It was a picture of two men and two women, all wearing bathing suits, inscribed "Lazy days at Lake Tahoe." The photo had been taken at a marina with a power cruiser in the immediate foreground showing Martha and Cindy Morgan in a smiling pose with two men. Very congenial group—it was hugs and smiles all around.

I passed the photo to the Chief and asked him, "Anyone here you recognize?"

He showed me a stiff smile as he replied, "Sure, but it must be a couple of years old. The men are Art Douglas and George Kaufman, Martha's first husband. I'm sure you have already identified the women."

I said, "Yeah. All but one of these are now dead. The fourth came damn close to joining the others a few hours ago. He's probably not out of the woods yet."

"I'm ready to get out of here," the Chief said. "It's giving me the willies."

I said, "Me too. Let's go."

We returned to the Chief's police car, where he ordered a unit dispatched to secure the crime scene. The dispatcher than reported, "We got a hit from CAL-ID on the hospital incident. Do you want the particulars now or are you on the way in?"

Terry gave me a pleased smile as he responded. "Feed me, Betty."

"First suspect identified as Rudolph Earl Marshan, D.O.B. August 4, 1948. Rap sheets in Florida, New York, Illinois, and California. Several arrests, attempted murder, no convictions. Two weapons violations, both reduced to misdemeanor offenses. Second suspect identified as Edward Charles Boschey, D.O.B. January 11, 1950. No criminal record. Honorable Discharge, U.S. Army, 1971. The car they were driving was stolen from a rental lot in South Lake Tahoe. That's the gist of it from CAL-ID, nothing yet from Washington, Chief."

"Ten-four. Good work, Betty. I'll be coming in as soon as the other unit arrives."

A few years ago it may have taken us weeks or months to obtain information like this, but modern police detection technology has become so advanced that local authorities can often access such information almost instantaneously. The California Identification Remote Access Network (CAL-ID) allows latent fingerprints to be injected into the system from virtually anywhere in the state and a list of potential matches can turn up within minutes. The use of police computer data-base systems has so revolutionized the identification and histories of suspects that often the officer on the beat, using a dashboard computer, can obtain a complete file on the suspect without even leaving his vehicle.

Terry left me alone for a moment while he stepped outside to confer with his arriving officer. Minutes later we were rolling toward the police department, a brief run from Old Mammoth. I asked about George Kaufman, reminding him of an earlier conversation that had touched briefly on the man.

I said, "The Tahoe connection keeps bothering me. First we had these two guys harassing Martha in the gallery and who probably should be considered the prime suspects for the torching of the gallery, then I find the same two searching Martha's condo. The two shooters at the hospital obviously came down from the same area. You told me that Sanford had a piece of the action at Tahoe and it appears that he is knee-deep in all of these recent events. How big a bite does he have?"

Terry replied, without actually looking at me, "Big enough to finance a number of his property development deals. He was a partner in one of the smaller casinos. Martha met Kaufman through her Dad, actually. Kaufman was his controller, the one who kept Harley's interests protected among the partnership. He had degrees in law and accounting. When you swim with sharks, it is wise to have a guy like Kaufman on top of the situation. That was his function."

"So Martha and Kaufman lived in Tahoe?"

"For a while. He was working for Harley when Martha met him. I had the feeling that it was not a particularly happy marriage."

"It looked happy enough in that photograph we found at Douglas's place."

"There had been a couple of separations before she moved back to Mammoth for good. She had lived here alone for some time before he was killed."

I said, "I know you're a good cop and this is a very small town, but I have to feel that you've had more than a casual interest in Martha's personal life."

The Chief said, "Yeah. Screw you too, bud. I've known Martha from way back. If you were trying to suggest something between Martha and me . . ."

I said, "Well, that got a rise. So what nerve did I touch there, pal?"

It had dawned on me for the first time that this guy was younger than I might have imagined and was probably something more than a mere police machine. I did not even know if the guy was married or had ever been—nothing personal about him. He did not rise to my bait so I punched him again. "Were you dating Martha before her marriage to Kaufman or after she moved back to Mammoth?"

He gave me a startled look. "God damn! You shoot from the hip, don't you, bud. Where did you get the idea I had dated Martha?"

I said, "Well, shit, you just confirmed it. Hey, I'm not

into the jealous-husband routine and I am not idiot enough to suppose that a beautiful and intelligent woman would not be attracted by the opposite sex. So get off it."

We were entering the parking lot at the police department when he chuckled and told me, "I've had a couple flings at the marriage game myself, so you're not talking to a choirboy here. Sure, I'd known Martha since before her first marriage and we'd had dinner a few times after she left Kaufman. We never got it on, if that's what you're wondering about, but not because I wouldn't have liked to. I guess we just sort of lost our moment. She was dealing with her divorce at the time and I knew that she was not ready to leap into another relationship right away. As a matter of fact, neither was I."

I asked, "So this was shortly before Kaufman was killed?"

"Yeah. The divorce wasn't final when he died."

"How did the trouble between Martha and her husband affect the relationship between Kaufman and Sanford?"

"Hell, I don't know. He was still working for Harley when he died. It would be characteristic of Harley to insist that those two work out their own problems without embroiling him. With Harley it has always been business first."

I said, "Even above his family, huh?"

"Oh, yeah. Harley's business deals have always been sacrosanct. You may have noticed that even his wife plays second fiddle to that."

"Yes, I had that feeling immediately. You hinted this morning that there may have been something fishy about the automobile accident that killed Kaufman."

"Yeah. It was on the Nevada side. I had no input there. The Nevada authorities were satisfied that it was a drunk-driving case. I never bought that. Kaufman was practically a teetotaler. Martha herself never bought it."

"Did Sanford buy it?"

He said, "You never know what a guy like Harley Sanford is buying and not buying. If you are asking if he seemed upset about his son-in-law's death—he never showed it."

It was growing more and more obvious that a trip to Lake Tahoe was shaping up for me, which would entail a three-hour drive north by car. But I was still a bit fuzzy behind the ears and I knew that my stamina was beginning to fade so I did not want to undertake a long trip by car before a bit of rest.

I mentioned this to the Chief as we got out of the car. He said, "Well, bud, I think we've both earned some rest. Myself, I'm bushed. You must be, too."

I knew it was true. I went on to my van and showed him a fond wave as he stepped inside the station.

I had really grown to like this guy.

I was thinking, as I moved into my van, that it would hurt like hell if this guy turned out dirty. It is not that I always look for the worst in people but that I have one of these sticky minds that is always affected by truths half spoken. Not that this guy had shown me any reason to distrust him—and I would love to believe that I could not have been affected by the possibility that he had been intimate with Martha—but only that something simply was not right here.

So maybe it was just fatigue.

I went back to the condo and hoped that I would have a different slant on things after a short rest. I should have known that any kind of rest was not in the cards for me that night.

# CHAPTER THIRTEEN

THE TELEPHONE WAS ringing as I walked into Martha's apartment. Chief Terry was on the horn. He said, "Janice Sanford is on my other line. Is it okay if I put her in touch with you?"

I asked, "Where is she calling from?"

"She's in L.A. She's having a problem with the release of Martha's body."

I said, "Sure, put her on."

Terry replied, "No, I can't patch her through, Joe. Are you feeling rummy?"

I told him, "Maybe I am. It's been a long day. Sure, tell her to call me. But do it quickly. I think I'm ready to crash at most any moment."

He said, "Okay, I'll tell her. Stay right there. She really needs to talk to you."

True to his word, the phone rang again almost immediately after we disconnected. Janice sounded none the worse for wear after the long trip into Los Angeles. She said, "I guess I did something dumb. I told the coroner's office that you were Martha's husband. Now they won't release the body to me. This is really dumb, isn't it?"

I told her, "That didn't occur to me, Janice. Is there someone I can talk with to straighten this out?"

She said, "You know it's really dumb how involved official red tape can be sometimes. But I guess it's my own fault. I didn't even bring the right paperwork with me. Martha Sanford did not exist anymore as a legal entity since the time she and George were married... and now that you two were married, it's even more complicated. This is a nightmare... and I don't think I can cope with it. I need your help, Joe."

"Where is your husband, Janice?"

"I don't know. I've rung the phone off the hook at home. I don't know where to go from here."

I said, "Looks like it's my problem, isn't it. Let me see if I can find someone to straighten this out for you. Give me the number you're calling from."

That fine reserve was beginning to crack at the edges as she replied, "I can order the company plane for you, Joe. It's only about an hour flight. Could you come down here?"

That was the last thing in the world I wanted to do. But it *was* my problem and I didn't see any way to avoid it. I told her, "Sure, I'll come. Tell me where to find the plane."

Her relief was obvious as she said, "Mammoth airport—you'll be meeting Tom Lancer. He's our pilot. I have already called ahead and made the arrangements at the airport. Tom will be ready as soon as you are."

I said, "Okay, I'll start immediately."

"Thank you, Joe. I know this is tough on you but I just didn't know what..."

"No, it's okay. Just sit tight. Why don't you wait for me in the hospital cafeteria? Have a bite to eat and stop worrying about it. I'm on my way."

So much for that. I called the Chief back and told him what was happening. He said gruffly, "Watch those big-city cops."

The cops were not my principal worry. I opened the secret compartment inside my van and sprung a 9mm Beretta from its concealing nook and strapped on the gun leather. I did not want to be unarmed again until this case was closed.

TOM LANCER SEEMED to be an okay guy. He came to greet me as I parked the van. "Are you Mr. Copp?"

I admitted it and he identified himself with crisp formality. A guy of about forty, lean and tanned, clean and well put together, with an aura of capable professionalism.

He already had the plane serviced and ready to fly—a Cessna Citation V jet, one of the newest of the fleet and impressively equipped for noncommercial service.

As we climbed aboard, Lancer told me, "I filed the flight plan for a fifty-minute flight to Burbank. That's about the best we're going to do in the vicinity of the hospital. Possibly we could find a closer field but it would be a difference of a few minutes at most, and many of the smaller fields have limited services. Mrs. Sanford will have a car waiting for you at the field."

I said, "Sounds great. You won't mind if I catch some sleep? I'm bushed."

He replied, "Not at all. There are refreshments and snacks if you're interested."

I thanked him and relaxed into my seat immediately. I don't even remember leaving the ground at Mammoth, and the arrival at Burbank was so smooth that I was a bit disoriented during the landing routine—I thought we were just taking off.

I had hoped that I might have a chance to talk to this guy about his boss during the flight but I doubt that it would have bought me anything, anyway. I did ask, just the same, while I was still half asleep and we were tax-iing toward the private terminal. "Did you take Mr. Sanford to Tahoe today?"

I got no response to that. Maybe he just did not hear me. The guy was busy and intent on handling the air-craft.

I asked him again when we arrived at the tie-down area and we stepped onto the field. Again he did not seem to hear the question. "Let's go see if your trans-portation is waiting for you, Mr. Copp."

That was obvious enough. Nothing particularly sur-prising about that—it was none of my business. I let it drop and we went into the terminal area.

A driver was waiting for me. I thanked the pilot and asked him, "Do you have instructions to wait for me here?"

He heard that one fine. "Yes, sir, Mrs. Sanford is ex-pecting to return to Mammoth with you."

I asked, "Are you aware of the nature of our business here?"

Lancer showed me a perplexed smile. "Yes, sir, I was told that we would be returning Mrs. Kaufman's body to Mammoth."

"When did you learn of Martha's death?"

"I learned about it when Mrs. Sanford called me this evening."

"Mr. Sanford had not told you?"

"I haven't seen Mr. Sanford since yesterday."

"Mr. Sanford did not call you a few hours ago for a flight to Tahoe?"

"I told you I haven't seen him since yesterday."

I said, "That is not what I asked you, Tom. Have you talked to Harley Sanford since yesterday?"

"No, sir."

"Why not? An expensive plane like that one just sits around on its wheels day after day? Isn't it your job to ferry the Sanfords around?"

The guy was losing patience with me. He said, "It is not my job, Mr. Copp, to tell people about my employer's business. So cut it out. If you want to know something about my employer, you're asking the wrong person."

I flashed my badge at him and asked, "Would this make any difference?"

He replied, "None at all. I knew you were a cop. That doesn't buy you anything in my store. I'm not trying to be unfriendly, and all my sympathies go to the entire family, but my first loyalty is to Mr. Sanford."

"Not to Mrs. Sanford?"

"I refer to both, of course."

"Did Mrs. Sanford tell you that Martha and I were married shortly before she died?"

That one hit home. For a moment it seemed that the man was going to call me a liar, but he recovered quickly and replied, "No, I didn't know about that. I'm sorry."

I told him, "It's a shocker, yeah. And maybe it's only the beginning of shock. Cindy Morgan was murdered today. Did you know that?"

That one seemed to hit him, too. "Cindy?" he gasped.

"Yes, and Arthur Douglas is teetering at the edge of death right now. He was shot, too. You didn't know that?"

"God, no!"

I said, "There has been an epidemic of violent death and it may not be over yet. Harley Sanford could be in deep trouble himself here. I'm not telling you this to scare you but to alert you to the situation. If Harley is in trouble, maybe he needs a friend right now more than anything else. Keep that in mind and maybe you'd like to discuss it further on the way home."

He said, in a slightly muffled voice, "I don't know what we'd have to discuss."

"What you're telling me is that you don't want to see and you don't want to know. That might not be enough to keep you out of trouble. My offer still goes."

The chauffeur of a waiting limousine had been patiently standing by. He seemed pleased that there was no luggage to be handled. Tom Lancer watched with interest as I followed the chauffeur to the door. He showed me a deferential smile and almost friendly wave as I walked out.

But there was more to it than that. I was sure that the guy wanted to tell me something. It was okay. I would have another shot at this one as we returned to Mammoth.


SOME MAY THINK that it was a bit foolhardy of me to venture back into the Los Angeles police jurisdiction at such a time, but actually I had known all along that those guys could have picked me up at any time of their choosing in Mammoth. That was not the bother. And I was not really all that bothered about another ordeal at the morgue. I was bothered, though, because I knew that all of my real problems were centered around Mammoth and it felt like I was in the wrong place at the wrong time.

If I have anything like a method to my police work, it involves an almost constant focus on the resolution of the problem. This flight to L.A. seemed to be a blunting of whatever edge I might have gained to this point. Not that I had a hell of a lot but at least I was more focused into the problem while in Mammoth than anywhere else.

All that aside, I knew that this was where I needed to be at this moment. Janice Sanford could have been in some real trouble of her own that had nothing whatever to do with the hassles she was encountering at the morgue. Something was out of kilter with her actions of the early afternoon—perhaps something entirely innocent but also maybe not. The feeling had been growing on me strongly that this was a family going into self-destruction. Obviously, Harley Sanford was in deep trouble. He, himself, was a very good candidate for a murder rap as well as attempted murder. I had to feel that somehow the death of Martha Kaufman was directly related to all the events of today.

I hoped that Janice Sanford was not involved in any of it. But I really did not feel any strong conviction about that. In fact, I think I was scared to death about what I might learn about my mother-in-law.

# CHAPTER FOURTEEN

Janice Sanford was tensely waiting for me just inside the door to the hospital cafeteria. She was immaculately dressed and coiffed but the day had taken its toll on her. Earlier I would have guessed this woman's age at around forty; at that moment she was looking much closer to her fifty-odd years.

She lit up when she saw me and hurried forward to embrace me. She said, "Thank you, Joe. I hate to seem like a ninny but I didn't know where to go with this."

I replied, "No, no, it's okay. We're family. I'm just sorry you had to be put through this."

"I was just having some coffee. Can I get you something?"

"That would help, sure—coffee's fine."

She replied, "Sit down. I'll get it."

I watched her getting the coffee and again it was almost like a flashback to a slightly older Martha, that same aura of grace and dignity under pressure. A casual observer would not have guessed that this was a heartbroken woman preparing to bury her only daughter.

She returned with the coffee and showed me a brave smile. "Sorry, I didn't remember how you take your coffee. I brought sugar and cream if you need it."

I thanked her and suddenly found myself at a loss for words.

There was a brief awkwardness as we stared at each other silently, then she sighed and said, "I have arranged for a mortuary to handle the details. They're waiting for our call once we get through the paperwork. We just need to complete the formalities here."

I wanted to spare her another trip through the morgue. I did not really want the coffee. "I'll go up and handle that. Are you comfortable here?"

"As comfortable as anywhere, I guess." Her relief was evident. "Thanks, Joe. Yes, if you don't mind, I'll just wait here."

I took the elevator to the second floor, and as I stepped out a feeling of dread began to grip me. I knew that they would insist that I view the body again. I had been through this kind of routine so many times before as a cop on duty, so it was not that I was unprepared for the experience, but of course this time I did not have the luxury of an impersonal encounter or the shelter of amnesia. I knew this victim now, and I had no effective defenses. My first viewing had done a number on me, even though I was largely out of my mind at the time. Now I knew that it was going to be brutal. I managed to shake it off and do what had to be done.

It was mercifully quick and done with a minimum of red tape. I provided all the necessary paperwork; the rest was routine. I told the attendant that I would notify the mortuary for the pickup. I signed an itemized list of her personal effects, stuffed the small bag into my pocket, and got out of there.

I returned to the cafeteria and told Janice, "Okay, it's

over. So now we just need to contact the mortuary and find out when we might expect them."

She told me, "The mortuary assured me that there will be no delay. The man knows that we're taking her home by private plane."

She was heading toward the telephone before I could offer to make the call myself. She had been through quite an ordeal. I knew that she wanted to get out of here as quickly as I did.

We were more than in-laws now.

The commonality of tragedy had given us something more intimate than mere kinship.


MARTHA'S BODY WAS not in a casket. Because of the relatively cramped quarters of a small airplane such as this one, the decision had been made to transport the remains in an iced body bag. There is a feeling of immediacy to such an arrangement. Janice had not wanted the body transported in the cargo hold, so it was placed in the aft cabin and securely strapped down. It was not as though we were in any intimate contact with the body. This particular configuration of the Cessna Citation was quite roomy. The passenger cabin was more than seventeen feet long, with seven comfortable seats, an executive table on each side, a lavatory aft, and a refreshment center forward. That was immediately where I headed. I knew that Janice needed a stiff drink and so did I.

I was glad that I had gone with her. This would have been a brutal trip for any mother and especially on her own. Tom Lancer came back to see that we were com-

fortable then went to the rear to double-check the security of the body. As he returned, he affectionately
squeezed Janice's shoulder. She squeezed him back and
I was afraid for a moment that she was about to cry.
This affected Lancer; his eyes were moist as he returned
to the cockpit and began his preflight check.

I guess this was the first time I had actually noticed
this aircraft and I was impressed by how far private air-
planes had come since the early days of noncommercial
aviation. The Citation was sleek and obviously at a high
state of the art. Of course, the price tag of a business jet
like this one was also light-years away from the little
single-prop Cessnas of not so many years ago. Apparently, Sanford had been doing well in his business. A
plane like this costs in the neighborhood of five million
dollars. Not so long ago you could have bought a large
commercial jet for that price. Times have changed.

It seemed incredible that I had rolled into Bishop almost exactly twenty-four hours earlier under the same
full moon. I still had Molly's patchwork shielding the
gunshot wound behind the right ear. Amazingly, and to
Molly's credit, the patch job was holding well through
all the adventures of the day, and if anyone had noticed
the wound, there had been no comment except by Chief
Terry when I had brought it to his attention. I had felt
a little ridiculous about wearing the hat in public but I
guess it had served its purpose; no little kids had run
away from me, as far as I knew. I mention that now
because Janice apparently caught a glimpse behind the
hat and said to me, "My God, Joe, what happened to
your head?"

Maybe she had wondered if I had worn the hat even

in bed; she had never seen me without it. I had to level with her, even though the very mention of Martha's death was bound to be painful for her. I said, "I was shot at about the same time that Martha was shot. I've had a weird sort of amnesia about the events surrounding all of that."

"Why haven't I heard any of that?" she cried almost angrily.

"I guess I was discussing it with your husband while you were out of the room."

She said, "That man! I overheard the marriage part of it, but all that Harley mentioned—well, he sort of shouted it at me as he ran past—was that you were responsible for Martha's death. That is so typical of Harley, to be affected only by his own pain and to blame everyone else when he doesn't control a situation. I was furious with the bastard!"

"He said as much to me at the time, that he was holding me personally responsible. Which was okay, because I was feeling something of the same myself."

"But he shouldn't have said anything like that to you! I mean, my God, I know that Martha had to have been deeply in love with you. She had such a terrible experience with George and swore she'd never go through that again. Listen, Joe, I'm as heartsick as Harley is about this but I know that Martha must have found a very special love with you. I see it in you, too, and I cannot excuse my husband for his insensitivity with you."

She reached across the aisle and squeezed my arm with genuine warmth. I patted her hand and said, "For what it's worth, Janice, I was in about the same situation that Martha was. I thought that marriage for me at this point in my life was out of the question. I would have married Martha only because I was crazy in love with her and could not have conceived of living without her. I have to be honest with you about this. Something got scrambled in my head when I took that bullet, and I'm having disturbing lapses of memory. To this moment I have no memory of the circumstances surrounding Martha's death. I told your husband that I would find the person responsible for it. Not that this may provide a lot of comfort to you but I am making that vow to you, too, right now."

She said, "Thanks, Joe. I want that, too. If money is any object..."

"Thanks. I doubt that money will ever be an object in this. I will find the killer and find justice for Martha."

Janice cried. It was the first tear I had seen from her. I leaned over and kissed her on the cheek and tried to comfort her. But the tears were a good sign. The emotional release was healing at such times. After a moment she whispered, "I'm so weary, Joe. I think I'll nap for a moment."

I released my seat belt and stepped across to recline her seat and adjust a small blanket for her comfort. She was half asleep already. I went forward to the cockpit and slid into the copilot's seat beside Lancer.

He had completed his preflight check and was talking to the tower for takeoff clearance when I joined him. Lancer was obviously absorbed with his work but he shot me a welcoming glance as we began taxiing into position toward the runway. We must have hit a seam in the traffic because we were cleared for takeoff immediately.

I don't care how many times you've seen this drama from a passenger seat, it's always a bit of a rush when the plane begins its takeoff roll. This was an even more dramatic experience from the cockpit. It was a hot plane and the cockpit instrument panel had a star-wars look. This guy was a veteran jet pilot, no doubt about that. We were flashing along the runway and lifting off faster than I would have thought possible. I had been around planes long enough to know that the takeoff is one of the most critical points of the flight; we were clear and climbing rapidly above Los Angeles with no discernible vibration. This plane was smooth as silk. I did not even hear the landing gear retracting but I could see the indication on the instrument panel. We were passing over the Mt. Wilson area almost immediately and climbing toward the stars.

Lancer leveled off to cruising altitude and activated the automatic pilot. It was the first opportunity that we had to talk. He asked me, "Have you done much flying?"

I said, "Not this way. How does a guy like Harley Sanford buy into a rig like this?"

He showed me a droll smile as he replied, "I guess it's not so hard if you know all the angles. This plane is used a lot and it's solid write-off."

"What is it used for?"

"Sanford has many business interests. Mostly development deals throughout the western states. It's a legitimate write-off. He couldn't run his business without this kind of instant hands-on availability."

"So he does travel a lot?"

"Well, no, not that much personally, not anymore. We use the plane more to shuttle the engineers and architects to the various company sites. Occasionally, we might run prospective clients around."

This guy had opened up a lot since our first conversation. Originally he had been cool almost to the point of rudeness. So now it seemed that he was looking at things with a different slant. He was downright friendly. I said, "Thanks for leveling with me, Tom. I won't pretend that I understand everything that has been going on in Mammoth, but I do feel strongly that Sanford may be in beyond his depth here—or that someone may be trying to make it appear that way. I'm going to lay this on you, straight and brutal. An all-points bulletin has been issued by the Mammoth police and Sanford is a prime suspect in two shootings over the past few hours. That is why I was interested in his whereabouts. I wasn't just trying to pump you for gossip. The man is in deep trouble. So if you have any information that may shed some light on the problems, you shouldn't think of it as an invasion of your employer's privacy."

He gave me an almost sardonic smile and said, "Yes, I got that message earlier. I don't want to discuss it right now, but it's food for thought and maybe I would like to talk to you about it after we get home."

I was feeling better about the guy when I returned to my seat.

Janice was sleeping soundly. According to my calculation we would be on the ground in Mammoth in less than a half hour. It was the first quiet chance I'd had to go through Martha's personal effects from the morgue.

It was a shocker when it occurred to me that her life had been reduced to this paltry inventory. There was a finely drawn gold necklace, which I had no memory of, a gold cigarette lighter engraved with the name Martha Kaufman, a simple gold wedding band inscribed, "Martha and Joe Forever"—which hit me like a ton of bricks, and the memory of placing it on her hand was like a knife twisted into my heart—and, finally, as though it had been carefully woven for my personal attention, a wide gold bracelet with a large cameo design. The bracelet had an almost antique quality. I kept working it through my fingers as though some rare secret was awaiting my discovery. And suddenly it revealed itself. I was twisting a gold clasp that adorned the underside when suddenly it sprang open. Inside was concealed a thin metal key with no identifying marks. It appeared to be a safety-deposit-box key. It would have fit unobtrusively inside a videocassette case or some similar common object, so maybe now I knew what had been the object of the search in Arthur Douglas's apartment—and/or the interest in Martha's condo.

For God's sake!

Had this "bauble" been the reason for Martha's death?

# CHAPTER FIFTEEN

I WAS FEELING guilty because I had done such a lousy job of pulling the pieces of this puzzle together. So many markers had been there from the very beginning but I had not been thinking like a cop. I should have known right from the start that something was sour with this whole thing. Martha's death had not been an incidental, unrelated event. Someone had killed her for an important purpose. Violent death is always the result of a chain of events that are related to cause and effect. Any cop knows that. Doesn't take a great brain to figure it out. Even the most casual drive-by shooting is wound somehow into a complex series of events that culminate in a violent death. So I was not too proud of the way I had conducted myself during the events of this day. Like I said, I had not been thinking like a cop—I had been thinking like a victim, I guess.

I should have known immediately that the burglary of Martha's condo was directly related to her murder. One of the things that had thrown me off early on was the family connection with Harley Sanford. This was greatly compounded by the possible involvement of Sanford in the shooting of Officer Douglas and later the death of Cindy Morgan. Then the apparent disappearance of Sanford following the discovery of the girl's body in his car added a bizarre twist to the chain of events. The torching of the Kaufman Gallery, although occurring out of sequence, was almost like a footnote to the entire improbable scenario, which actually could have begun with the questionable death of George Kaufman two years earlier.

This retrospection was interrupted by Lancer's announcement over the P.A.: "Touchdown in ten minutes."

That roused Janice. She showed me a wan smile and said, "I needed that nap—thanks."

I discreetly slipped Martha's bracelet into my coat pocket and said to Janice, "Are you fully awake?"

"I think so."

"I have been wondering about the relationship between Martha and her family."

"What do you mean?"

"I am curious why we'd never met until today."

She gave me an embarrassed smile. "Things had not been good between Martha and her father for quiet some time. He was devoted to her, but I'm afraid that he always treated Martha like a personal possession. It had not been good between them since her estrangement from George Kaufman. Harley took that as a personal affront."

"Things were tight between George and Harley?"

"Not that so much. George was handpicked by Harley to be Martha's husband. I always felt that Martha looked at the marriage as more of a convenience for Harley than for her own personal happiness. Frankly, I could never blame Martha for feeling that way. It was about as close to a shotgun wedding as you could find."

"So what did this do to your relationship with Martha?"

She sighed and said, "I have never been proud of the way I caved in to my husband on this matter. I have always been a terrible coward when it comes to going against my husband's wishes. What this says about me I cannot defend. I guess I've always had an old-school attitude about marriage. Of course that has always made it very easy for Harley to dominate me. I'm not proud of that either. But no more. Maybe Martha would be alive today if I hadn't been such a pushover." She was weeping without embarrassment.

I couldn't let her give herself such a bad rap. I reached over and tried to comfort her. "Martha is dead, Janice, because of events far beyond your ability to influence them." I produced the bracelet and showed her the hidden key. "I have a feeling that this is why Martha died. Have you ever seen this before?

With hardly a glance at the bracelet she said, "Yes, I gave it to her myself when she was eighteen. It belonged to my mother. How could that have had anything to do with Martha's death?"

Obviously she had not noticed the safety-deposit key. I gave her a closer look at the key and said, "Not the bracelet, Janice. The key. Do you recognize this?"

"Yes, I have one just like it. Not the same key, I'm sure, but they all look alike."

"Safety-deposit?"

"Yes." She took the key and inspected it more closely. "Looks just like mine."

"Your bank in Mammoth?"

"Yes."

I said, "It could be important. Did you know that Martha had a safety-deposit box?"

"No, I didn't. But Martha had been in business on her own since her separation from George. She has been totally self-sufficient for the past few years."

"Did Harley help her start the gallery?"

"No. Not that he wouldn't, but she wouldn't have allowed it. Martha was not like me, Joe. She was fiercely independent of her father after she got out of that disastrous marriage. She would not have given Harley another opening like that. Anyway, I know that Martha started that gallery with her own money. She didn't need Harley's money. George's life insurance, while not particularly lavish, left her quite comfortable. For the first time in her life she didn't need her father for anything. I think that's what disturbed him so."

I became aware of a rapid descent at about the time that Lancer reported, "Let's get buttoned down. Beginning our approach." He added, "Joe, would you like to come up front for a better view?"

Janice said, "Why don't you, Joe? I've seen this many times."

I thanked her and went on forward to join the pilot.

It was a spectacular sight. You don't capture the full beauty of this area from the ground. I had never seen it this way, and even under these unhappy circumstances I was almost transfixed by the view from the cockpit. The moon was still high and bright in the sky, illuminating the snowcapped peaks. Lancer masterfully dropped the jet toward the mountain valley and we were suddenly surrounded by numerous shimmering lakes dotting the mountain basins below.

Poor bastards, as Chief Terry was wont to say. None of us had an inkling of the terror that was awaiting us in this tranquil setting.

"THIS WILL BE a straight-in approach," Lancer told me with cool confidence. "This is not a controlled airport, so there won't be anyone around at this time of night. I notified the mortuary of our time of arrival, so the hearse should be waiting at the field."

"There's no FAA here?"

"No. There's a remote radio access to the flight-service station at Riverside, but that's a trunk line setup with limited hours and even then it may be subject to delay."

"Straight-in approach to what? Where the hell's the airport?"

Lancer said, "Good question. This is slick. Watch this, it's a pilot-controlled lighting system." He quickly keyed the mike button five times. High-intensity strobe lights, like a thousand Roman candles, blazed alive and created a perfect runway configuration like a highway to heaven.

Moments later, Lancer was expertly threading the needle, softly massaging the craft into the illuminated pathway. Just before touchdown he quickly keyed the mike again, dimming the runway lights and activating the runway-end identifier lights. An instant later, we were setting down and he hit the thrust-reversers. I could feel the G-forces as the hurtling aircraft went into a smoothly controlled deceleration.

I had noticed a stationary Jeep alongside the runway

with two standing figures silhouetted behind the windshield as Lancer taxied into the turn at the end of the landing roll. This was no hearse and I could see no reason for these guys to be out here. I yelled, "This looks like unexpected company and these don't look like lovers, pal."

Lancer was busy executing his turn onto the taxiway but he had caught it, too. He said, "Shit, I think those guys have guns."

It was like a prophecy. I couldn't hear the gunfire but I could see the flashes from two high-powered rifles laying in on us—and this was no prophecy. These bastards were shooting at us.

Lancer yelled, "Hell, we're taking fire!"

So we were. A volley of heavy bullets smacked through the windshield and shredded the interior cabin walls behind us. Lancer was no dummy; I got the idea very quickly that this guy had been in combat situations before. He was maneuvering to get clear when the nose wheel exploded and sent us into a shuddering skid. He said coolly, "Christ, if they hit a fuel tank...!" He instantly killed the engines as the plane collapsed onto the forward gear.

I heard Janice yell out in alarm. We were sitting ducks! Those bastards were no more than fifty yards away from us. Lancer sprung a .45 automatic from his seat pocket at the same instant I unholstered my Beretta and said, "I have to get Janice out of here."

Lancer yelled, "I'll try to cover you. Use the escape hatch." He already had his gun extended through the small window opening beside the pilot's seat. He was blasting away when I rushed back to lead Janice out.

I released her seat belt and said, "We're getting out of here."

She hesitated and glanced toward the rear of the cabin. "Martha . . ."

"Not now." I unlatched the release lever on the emergency exit and pulled Janice out of the seat. "Keep close," I warned her.

Lancer was plenty sharp, okay. He was keying the mike to turn the blinding strobe lights on and off while we made our escape from the plane. Brave guy. He knew that the plane could go up in a ball of flame at any moment. Meanwhile, he was keeping the shooters busy with his return fire from the cockpit.

This was heroic shit. I had the greatest admiration for this guy as he maintained his post, braving almost certain death. I carried Janice clear and deposited her in a shallow ditch beside the runway. "Stay down!" I told her, and went back to support Lancer.

Maybe it hadn't been conscious on his part at the time but what had saved our butts from the opening gunfire was the way Lancer had positioned the craft away from the line of fire. The shooters had not calculated the length of the Citation's shorter landing roll and they were not in the proper position to target their fire effectively. They had really expected the plane to utilize much more of the runway and they were tucked in for a duck shoot directly opposite their position. Lancer defeated their plan when he unexpectedly wheeled around for his return to the hangar area. Off balance and firing at a difficult angle, they missed their chance.

When Lancer hit the strobes again, this must have blinded them momentarily and his surprise return fire added to their confusion.

It was a continuing hot firefight. I was really firing more for show than for effect as I sprinted back to the emergency exit. Luckily, the return fire now seemed disorganized and largely ineffective.

My strongest instinct was to go after those guys, but the pressing worry was the vulnerability of the plane to explosion and Lancer's imminent danger. His pistol had suddenly fallen silent. All of this action had spanned a minute at most. Life and death are often measured by such brief moments totally out of context with ordinary time; to a burning man, a split second must seem like an eternity. A fight like this can be similar. In the recounting of such events, real time has no measure.

I dived back into the plane and yelled at Lancer. "Let's get out of here!" I went to the rear and fought Martha's body clear of the restraining harness and yelled again, "Tom, let's go!"

He replied painfully, "I'm hit!"

I slid the body bag off the plane and Lancer was right behind me. He'd taken a shoulder hit and was losing blood fast. I ordered him, "Wrap that up with something," and pushed him in the direction of the ditch. To the credit of this guy, he used his good arm to help me drag the body clear. Just in time—one of the shooters had just closed on the disabled plane and was trying to get an angle for a close shot.

I got there first.

I rolled under the plane and fired once at point-blank

range. The Beretta shivered the guy and sent him careening backward.

The other shooter must have spotted his partner go down; he opened up a furious barrage toward the aircraft. The guy seemed to be targeting the fuel tanks in the wings.

I had to discourage that.

To my dismay, I had nothing to discourage it with. The clip of my Beretta was empty.

# CHAPTER SIXTEEN

I WAS ROLLING clear of the target area with all possible haste. Lancer was aware of my predicament. He yelled, "Joe!" and slid his gun across the pavement toward me. This guy must have had a great bowling average. The gun slid right into my outstretched hand. He had a fresh clip in the .45. I popped off the safety, slid the hammer back, and chambered in a round. Just in time, too. The other guy was still having some trouble with the strobes; the lights were giving him fits and I suspected that he was firing almost blindly. My line of sight was perfect and I felt that I must have hit the guy with one of my first few rounds because he quickly lost heart for the fight. I heard him gunning the engine of the Jeep and trying for a hasty withdrawal. The way the Jeep was lurching forward I had the impression that this guy had never driven a stick shift and it was giving him a problem. He had to restart the engine twice and was kicking up a cloud of dust in his frantic attempts to get away.

I immediately anticipated the guy's intent to break toward the Owens River Road leading back to U.S. 395, which parallels the airport runway. I went off on a dead run, expecting to intercept him before he could reach the highway, which was pure faith on my part because at the time I had only the vaguest idea of the surrounding terrain. I guess I just got lucky. Twice I lost my footing on the uneven turf as I scrambled to beat him to the intersection with the highway. Fortunately I was not the only one having difficulty. The Jeep was still jerking along the road in first gear when I broke clear of the airport proper. I could see the panic in this guy's response as he spotted me beside the road—he was a dead duck and he knew it, but still he tried to just blow on through. He was fighting to get his rifle in position when I massaged a single deadly round from the .45. The big bullet blew the guy out of the vehicle and beneath it as it heeled abruptly, climbed the shoulder, and flipped over.

I discovered later that it was not the gunshot that was directly responsible for his death; he had suffered a broken neck when the Jeep rolled over him. Also, there was a nick from another bullet, which confirmed my earlier suspicion that I had winged him before his withdrawal.

The important thing from my point of view was that the shooting had ended with the plane still intact. Of course it had suffered quite a bit of damage.

Vehicles from two police agencies, the Sheriff's Department and the Highway Patrol, arrived on the scene while I was returning to the airport proper. An ambulance was dispatched for Tom Lancer. Janice had been made comfortable in the front seat of the sheriff's unit and seemed to be none the worse for the experience.

A shaken mortician's assistant had been an eyewitness to the startling events. The hearse had been standing-by near the tie-down area when the plane landed. It was he who had alerted the police when the shooting began.

It was at this point that one of the police units from Mammoth P.D. arrived although the airport was several miles outside the city. This is more or less standard procedure to offer mutual assistance between agencies at such times. A firefighting unit had also been dispatched from somewhere nearby but they were not needed here. It reminded me, though, of how close we all had come to a disastrous situation on the field.

The mortician took charge of Martha's body and an ambulance from Mammoth hurried Tom Lancer to the hospital for treatment of his wound. He was okay, it seemed, except for a flesh wound in the upper arm, which might have been a severe problem if Janice had not been there to render effective first aid on the spot.

All in all, we had gotten off lucky. We all knew it and even the guys from the fire department were marveling at our close call. The airport operator arrived and took charge of the plane for towing to the hangar area. He, too, kept reminding me how lucky this all worked out.

It took an hour to get all the police reports satisfied and the two dead hoods collected and transported to the morgue. Chief Terry showed up at some point in this process, showed me a sympathetic smile, and said, "You've had a busy day, bud."

I tiredly replied, "Yeah, tell me about it."

He volunteered to take Janice home and I happily acceded to that suggestion. It was about two-thirty A.M. when I collected my van and headed back into Mammoth. I must have picked up a second wind or something because I was feeling more alert and together inside my head than I had felt since my awakening in the hospital in Los Angeles some forty hours earlier.

Which was good, because there was no rest for me in the developing scenario of this night.

Like Goldilocks, someone was sleeping in my bed.

He had been a relative of mine briefly and now he was a fugitive on the run.

Harley Sanford was fast asleep in my bed.


I BELIEVE I would not have liked this guy under any circumstances. He was not one of those warm individuals who immediately inspire friendship. If I had encountered him in a normal family situation, I still would have had trouble with this guy. But for Martha's sake, and maybe for Janice's sake, I may have been inclined to make allowances and at least try to create the fiction of a friendly family connection.

But this was not the same man I had met a few hours earlier. The superior air, the guile, the toughness—all of that was gone when this obviously broken man sat up in the bed and cried, "Thank God, you're here! I was afraid I had missed you. Listen, I'm in deep trouble. I need your help."

He was fully clothed, even to his shoes, an afghan draped over him for warmth against the chill night air.

I asked, "Where have you been, Harley?"

He said, "Christ, it's cold in here. What time is it?"

I said, "It's time to get your ass out of my bed," and I went to the kitchen. I started a pot of coffee and waited for him to get himself together.

I heard him in the bathroom and he emerged a moment later. He had splashed water on his face and had not bothered to towel off. He looked like hell. This guy had *been* in hell. He said quietly, "I could use some of that coffee."

"In a minute," I said.

He took a seat at the table and seemed to be trying to put his thoughts together. "This has been a nightmare. I've been waiting for you for hours. Do I understand correctly that you are a private investigator?"

"That's right," I replied coldly.

"I think I'm in a lot of trouble. I want to retain you."

"For what?"

"For whatever it is private eyes do. You don't seem to understand. I told you I'm in deep trouble."

I said, "A hundred thousand a day wouldn't help you, pal. What you need is a lawyer—a damned good criminal lawyer. But just for fun, what is it you would expect me to do for you?"

He asked, "Isn't that coffee done yet?"

I told him, "Another minute. Coffee can't give you that much comfort. You look like a man in need of a strong drink."

"What do you have?"

"I think Martha kept a bit of wine around here."

"Thanks, I'll stick to the coffee." He stood up and helped himself to the unfinished brew.

I get aggravated with people who do that. But this was obviously one of those guys short on patience and disdainful of proper process.

He asked, "Where's your cup?"

"You've got it," I said. "Never mind, I'll wait."

"Did you hear me? I want to retain you."

"You told me that. I asked you, for what?"

"I think someone has been trying to kill me."

I said, "Here's a flash for you, pal. There's been an epidemic of violent death here lately. A little over an hour ago, someone tried to kill your wife. Is that of any interest to you?"

His normally wary look was reasserting itself. He took a pull at his coffee. "Why would anyone want to kill Janice?"

I told him, "That's the same thing I've been asking myself. I guess you're a prime contender. Do you know that the Mammoth police have issued an all-points bulletin on you?"

He seemed genuinely mystified by that statement. "Why, for God's sake?"

I said, "That's the usual procedure when the police are trying to apprehend a murder suspect."

"Wait." His native caution was fully intact now. "You've got it wrong. I am the victim, not a suspect!"

"You didn't shoot Arthur Douglas?"

"Arthur! Why would I shoot Arthur?"

I asked him, "Why would you shoot Cindy Morgan?"

His face was a total blank. I almost felt sorry for this guy until he continued to stonewall it. He said, "I don't know what you're talking about."

"She's dead," I replied without emotion.

Sanford growled, "No, wait, you mean Martha, don't you?"

"No, I'm talking about Cindy," I said coldly.

"Is everyone crazy around here?"

It was nearly the same reaction I got from this guy

when I told him about his daughter's death. There was no real sense of sadness or even regret—only anger, maybe, and self-pity. I said, "I'm going to give it to you level, Harley. Feel free to jump in here any time I'm telling you something that you already know." I told him about the string of shootings, leaving nothing unsaid that needed saying.

As I recited that litany of horror, Sanford listened without comment until finally he groaned, "You wouldn't lie about this kind of stuff?"

I said, "I have better things to do with my time." I showed him Martha's bracelet. "Is this what your boys were looking for here yesterday?"

The guy was still playing it cagey. "What is that?"

"Your wife gave this bracelet to Martha years ago. It means nothing to you?"

"What is it supposed to mean?"

I said, "I'm trying very hard, Harley, to be civil with you, but if you insist on playing games with me I'll toss your ass outside."

"I'm not playing games," he protested. "I've never seen this before."

I produced the safety-deposit key. "This is not what your boys were searching for in here yesterday?"

I got a reaction on that one. "Where did you find that?"

I said, "Martha was wearing this the day she was killed. Is this what killed her?"

I guess that was cruel, but it wasn't intended that way. I was simply trying to unravel the puzzle. He stared at me through a long, incredulous moment then collapsed onto the table. He began sobbing. There was not much to offer this man as consolation. I had the unkindest suspicion of all, that this guy was weeping over only his own misfortune. I got up and went into the living room to give him some privacy with his grief, although to tell the truth I was not sure that he was entitled to that.

Sanford had crashed on the bed again when I went back to look in on him. I did not consider that particularly surprising. It had been a long, hard day for both of us. He opened his eyes and showed me a defeated grimace. I said, "I'll bunk in the other room. We will need to straighten out this mess with John Terry at first light. So get yourself together. I'll go in with you in the morning."

I was not sure that he had heard or understood what I was saying. I knew that I should have tried to resolve all this here and now, but I was just too beat, myself, to attempt to bring all these pieces into focus.

I should have tried harder. Come sunrise, I was going to hate myself.

# CHAPTER SEVENTEEN

**I** HAD NEVER been one to spend a lot of time in bed—sleeping. I had always resented unconscious time. Often, when working on a case, I would work several nights straight through with only an occasional brief respite to keep me running. But of course, this time, I had not been fully myself and I should have known that. I was still sound asleep on the couch when Chief Terry called me at a few minutes past eight.

He said, "Time to rise and shine, bud. You planning on sleeping all day?"

I groaned, "Oh, shit. I had wanted to get up early. Thought I had set the alarm." I was inspecting the alarm clock as I told him that. Hell, the alarm had been turned off. I growled, "Hold it just a second."

I dropped the telephone and hurried into the bedroom. My pigeon had flown the coop.

I went back to the phone and told Terry, "Well, I blew it. Sanford was in my bed when I got back last night. Dammit!—the guy was confused and wanting help. I should have called you immediately."

He asked, "He's not there now?"

"No. I believe that he sabotaged my alarm clock. So I have no idea—"

"I'm not surprised. Harley had a busy night. Why don't you get over here as quick as you can. We've got visitors."

I said, "I'll need ten minutes to get clear. Have the coffee ready."

"You got it," he replied as he hung up.

It was characteristic of this guy to waste no time crying over spilled milk. Some cops I have known would have been reading the riot act over my failure to apprehend a wanted suspect. There was none of that stuff in this guy.

I invaded the shower and tried to clear my head of the cobwebs. The hit at the airport had an almost surreal quality, and I was trying to put the events into a clear perspective that made some sense but the steaming water was doing little to accomplish that.

Had the gunmen at the airport been trying to kill me ... or someone else? If me, who could have been that worried about my involvement in the problems here? If not me, that left only Janice Sanford and Tom Lancer, and a girl already dead, aboard that plane. So what the hell was it all about?

The gunmen had undoubtedly been launched by the same people who had hoped to silence Arthur Douglas ... but why had he needed silencing? What could a small-town cop add to the mystery that would be worth the risk of a daring execution-style slaying in open view of a score of witnesses?

As for that business at the airport, what could have been the motive and why was it so important?

And maybe I had just missed the most obvious implication. Harley seemed to think that someone had been trying to kill *him.* So maybe that was true, and maybe the gunmen at the airport had expected Harley Sanford to be aboard.

And if Harley had been the target all along, as he seemed to have thought, how would that account for the gunmen at the hospital?

Whatever, I had to get moving, so I got out of there as quickly as possible. I was at the P.D. fifteen minutes later. There was something similar to a war conference underway in the Chief's office. Official brass from two different sheriff's departments and a contingent from the California Highway Patrol were discussing the crime spree in this placid mountain village.

Terry performed introductions all around. I had met one of the highway patrolmen briefly several years earlier but I did not immediately recall the circumstances. His name was Griffith and he reminded me that we had met at a police convention in Sacramento. He said, with a genial smile, "Figured you were dead or in jail years ago, Joe."

I gibed back with a smile, "That could apply to every man in this room. So what's new in your world?"

Griffith chuckled as he replied, "Same old, same old. Who tried to take your head off?"

Molly's patch job had fallen apart in the shower. I had tried to glue it back together but one end kept waving in the breeze every time I moved, so I ripped the whole thing off and tossed it into a wastebasket. I asked him, "Why do I have the feeling that you already have the answer to that?"

He grinned and said to the group at large, "Copp has always been good for a laugh when things get boring."

But no one else seemed to be laughing and certainly there was no hint of boredom in this particular crowd. Two of these guys were showing almost open contempt for my inclusion in this group. That was not particularly surprising. As a private eye I had long since been aware of open hostility from cops as soon as they knew my history. Which is not to be taken personally; very often cops from different official quarters do not get along well even with one another. I usually try to put the disrespect in perspective and try to take no offense. That can be difficult at times. I had this group pretty well sized up the moment I walked in there. To some cops, a private eye is scum, no matter how you may prove them wrong. I stopped trying long ago.

Chief Terry said, almost as though to lighten up an overcharged atmosphere, "I want it known right up front here that this guy saved my butt yesterday afternoon, so I expect him to be accorded all the respect that I demand for myself. If anybody here can't handle that, there's the door."

I took it by that comment that Terry had been getting some static about me from these guys.

One of the sheriff's people, a guy named Armstrong, was trying to put a good face on the discussion. He smiled at Terry and said, "I have no problem with that."

Another cop said, "Me neither."

At least no one got up and walked out.

But it seemed that the conference had sputtered to an end. I had the feeling that these people had come just to get a day out of the office anyway; and it would probably look good in the political arena. What could these guys accomplish, after all, except to embellish public

relations between police agencies. The individual pa-
trolman or detective out on the streets is the man who
makes the crucial difference every time, not the brass.
At the bottom line, police work usually comes down to
an individual cop on the beat face-to-face with a criminal. You cannot get more basic than that, and the individual cop has to know that he cannot depend on
anyone except himself in a moment of crisis. Any cop
who forgets that is in extreme jeopardy. There are a lot
of badass people out on these streets—anywhere, everywhere.

I stepped outside for a breath of air as the meeting
broke up. Griffith came out and shook my hand again.
He said, "Terry there is a good man. He seems to be in
your corner at the moment but don't give this guy too
much slack. Watch yourself, Joe."

I said, "Thanks. I always try to keep my back to the
wall but I have seen this guy under fire and I respect
him. Beyond that, yeah, I hardly know the man. Were
you trying to tell me something I ought to know?"

He chuckled and lowered his voice as he replied, "I
just said it."

I said, "No, I think you didn't."

"How long since you've been to Tahoe?"

"Is that a suggestion?"

"I've heard things. Maybe you should."

I said, "Thanks, it's on my schedule."

He showed me a cryptic smile and went on.

So what the hell was that about? Some of these people
often end up a bit paranoid, so I was not particularly
impressed by the apparent warning.

But a jaunt to Tahoe was definitely looming larger in

my immediate future. If, that is, I had any future left.

For the moment, however, I wanted a private conversation with John Terry regarding his old pal, Harley Sanford.

I had to call it that way.

The guy had simply been too tolerant of his leading citizen's possible involvement in the violence of yesterday.


TERRY MET ME outside and said, "Let's go find some breakfast."

When we got into his car I asked him, "What was so hot on your mind when you called me a while ago?"

"No, you first. What's this about Harley?"

I told him, "I gave it to you. He was in my bed when I got home last night. I figured he would keep until morning. He didn't."

"So what was on his mind?"

"He seemed stunned that he might be a murder suspect. He was confused and scared. He didn't admit to anything but he also didn't deny anything."

"That sounds typically Harley. But what was your sensing of what he said?"

I said, "My sensing was that the guy was scared out of his skull. Where are we going?"

We were moving slowly along Old Mammoth Road. The Chief replied, "They have a good breakfast at The Swiss Cafe. It's just down the street. Like waffles?"

"Whatever," I said. "What is your startling news about Sanford? You said something on the phone about him having a busy night. What was that?"

"Waffles first," he said.

I could tell that he wasn't just stalling me but was working at something inside his own head. I allowed him to nurse it until we were seated in the restaurant. But that took a while too. This guy had a lot of friends. We had to run the gamut of interested queries on the big news around town, and he was not one to be churlish with the local folks. As soon as we got that all settled down and breakfast ordered, he told me, "I talked to Harley last night, too. He said that someone had been trying to kill him and that he was afraid to show himself until I could guarantee his safety."

"What time was that?"

"That was close to midnight. I tried to convince him that we needed to straighten out his problems but he was hitting me about the same way he was hitting you, from what you told me."

I said, "Well, maybe I'm nuts but I really felt that the guy didn't know anything about the shootings. He was in a hell of a sweat. He was crying. I went in the other room to give him a chance to pull it together. When I came back he was bundled into bed again. I figured, what the hell, the guy would keep through the night. I was pretty well bombed out, myself. I've been wondering all morning why I didn't call you on the spot. But I can tell you this much, I felt no fear of this guy. I don't often tuck myself into bed with a murderer just down the hall from me. I've had to rethink this whole scenario. I can tell you this—"

I did not get the chance to tell him "this," whatever it was.

Terry's beeper summoned him at that point.

He excused himself and went to the telephone in the lobby.

I got about three good bites of a gorgeous Belgian waffle before he returned, with all illusions of a leisurely breakfast gone for sure.

"Let's go," he said urgently. "I'll tell you about it in the car."

It was not done, yet, in Mammoth.

Harley Sanford was dead.

# CHAPTER EIGHTEEN

THE BODY WAS lying just off the third green on the golf course. It had been there awhile, crumpled facedown near the top of a shallow sand trap. He'd been shot in the head and had apparently rolled down a hill into the bunker from a few yards above.

A revolver lay beside the body.

A note tucked inside a pocket of his pants appeared to be a suicide message.

The note said, simply, "I'm just too tired," and was unsigned.

Chief Terry had tears in his eyes. He said quietly, "That poor woman. Now she has another to bury."

That was exactly what he said, with no apparent concern for Harley himself. People do not always say precisely what is in their minds at such a time, but it struck me a little odd that all the sympathy had gone to the widow and none for the victim. But it was also no time to split hairs.

I told him, "I want to go with you to notify Janice."

He said, "Let's go right now, before she can hear it from someone else."

Other officers were on the scene. We left immediately,

and Terry was still brushing moisture from his cheeks as we sped away.

I was not buying this as a suicide. Not yet, anyway, and certainly not until all the other shootings had been reasonably explained. I wanted to try to find out where Sanford had been during the long hours since Cindy Morgan's death. If it could be shown that Harley Sanford had indeed been guilty of the murder of Cindy and/or the attempted murder of Arthur Douglas, then maybe something could be built of a suicide theory. At the moment, I was not buying it.

And I knew for sure, now, that I would have to make that trip to Lake Tahoe as soon as possible. There was no way to avoid the implications of a string of violence that probably began at least as early as the questionable death of Martha's first husband, George Kaufman.

I had to consider my own shooting, in L.A., as another link in the chain of violence, which had intensified dramatically after my return to the area, and of course that included also the Los Angeles shooting of Martha. All of the violence that had erupted around this family over the past couple of years had to be connected in some weave of cause and effect.

Sanford's connection to a criminal element was beyond question. "Sammy and Clifford," the small-time hoods who invaded Martha's apartment, acting on Sanford's orders by his own admission, makes that connection quite clear. That same or a similar connection certainly had figured in the torching of the Kaufman Gallery—but how, why, for what effect?

And of course I had to believe that somehow it was

all tied into the mysterious safety-deposit key that Martha had worn to her death. As an initial item of business, I would need to find what lay inside that box.

The criminal connection undoubtedly figured strongly in much of the intrigue of the past twenty-four hours or so, and probably from the beginning.

Who else would have killed Martha Kaufman and tried to kill me, either directly or indirectly? Who else had wanted to kill Arthur Douglas, twice? Who else had killed Cindy Morgan and who else had attacked an airplane and tried to snuff out three lives in a single stroke? And finally, now, what was really behind the death of Harley Sanford? Events such as these do not occur in a vacuum; it would be ridiculous for any cop to conclude that these were no more than a series of random events.

So, yes, I had to look into the Tahoe connection, if only to satisfy myself that nothing was there to account for all this violence.

And, of course, there had been the almost cryptic warning by Griffith following the meeting in Terry's office. Maybe he had just been shooting in the dark, as cops often do, but it could have been more than that.

So Tahoe was definitely on my schedule.

Not right away, though.

Someone had just tried to kill Janice Sanford again, this time with a heavy overdose of a narcotic drug.

The count was getting furious. And so was I.

THE PARAMEDICS WORKED with a professional and swift calm to stabilize the O.D. victim. You can't say too much about these people, who often are the only difference between life and death, and who are paid far too little for their efforts. Janice was quickly stabilized and en route to the hospital within minutes. I rode in the ambulance with her while Chief Terry stayed behind to await his investigating officers and see to the police reports. As I jumped into the ambulance, Terry showed me a dour grimace and growled, "This has gone too far, bud. We've got to put a cap on this crap!"

"Show me how," I growled back.

It was a quick run in to the hospital. Janice had been semiconscious the whole while but not lucid enough to explain the circumstances except to say that "they" had injected her "full of drugs." We had found her in a bathrobe staggering along the drive beside her house, apparently trying to get into her car. While waiting for the paramedics, Terry had discovered that her telephone line had been cut. Only her indomitable will had kept her functional and attempting to find help.

Both Terry and I felt that only our fortuitous visit to notify Janice of her husband's death had foiled the attempt on her life. Maybe this is a hell of a way to put it, but Janice was alive only because her husband was not.

I stood by in the emergency waiting room while the medics attended her. Terry arrived as I was being briefed by the attending physician. Janice was then out of danger. We also discussed Harley's death. The doctor advised that Janice not be told about that at this time.

Janice's condition seemed to relieve the chief of considerable anxiety, but he was mad as hell. So was I. I had known these people so very briefly, and I could not say that I had even liked Harley Sanford, but I was definitely taking the whole thing personally and I knew that Terry was too, even if his earlier reaction to Harley's death had seemed to be more centered on Janice's pain then on the death of an old friend.

The Chief and I went in for a brief visit with the patient. We stayed only a moment because she was in no condition to explain what had happened to her. She did not even ask about her husband but she did ask about Tom Lancer. She was receiving good care and seemed to be okay, so we left her and went to look in on the other victims.

Arthur Douglas had taken a "turn for the worse" and we were not allowed to question him. Terry left instructions that he wanted to speak with his officer at the first reasonable opportunity.

This small hospital seemed to be developing a "police wing" to accommodate the rash of crime victims. Douglas had remained in the intensive care ward under constant police guard, which was straining the capabilities of this limited police department. As an added precaution, both Janice and Tom Lancer were being cared for in rooms adjacent to the other victim to enable the police guard to keep tabs on all three.

It was shortly before eleven o'clock. Lancer was not in his room at the moment, receiving some kind of follow-up treatment for his arm wound preparatory to his release from the hospital. Terry was in a sweat to get back to his office so I suggested that he go on without me. I wanted a shot at Lancer on my own, anyway.

I followed the Chief outside and spoke to him through his car window as he was firing up. I asked him, "What did you learn about the shooters at the airport?"

"More or less what we expected to find," he replied. "These guys were professionals, like the other two here at the hospital yesterday. These two even advertised in a magazine."

"That's a bit different approach."

"Not anymore."

"Little bit different pedigree, though."

"The mobs come in all shapes and sizes now," he reminded me. "There are even Asian gangs working territories around the country now."

"These weren't Asians."

"I didn't say they were. The effect is the same. I think it's worse now than ever before. I don't know about you, bud, but I am sick and tired of these people coming in here and shooting up my town."

I said, "Sure, tell me about it. All it means is that it can happen here as easy as in Los Angeles, New York, and Chicago. A few lousy bucks will buy your dirty work anywhere these days. So Mammoth has come of age, that's all. You don't have to like it, but . . . "

"Bullshit. I'll never like it and I'll never go for it. Take book on that."

"Where'd these guys come from?"

"Believe it or not, they came from a little town in Texas. The Jeep was stolen from a military installation out of Hawthorne."

"Where's that?"

"It's in Nevada, dammit."

"Near Tahoe?"

"Not really. It's just northeast of here, out in the middle of nowhere."

"Casino action?"

"Has a couple of small casinos but the ammunition depot is the lifeblood there. Is that the end of your interrogation?"

I said, "Hey, pal, don't get testy with me. I'm on your team."

"I know, I know," he growled, and went on without further comment or apology.

He was getting pissed, yeah. But that did not change anything and it did not fix anything.

I wanted that talk with Tom Lancer. And then I wanted to look in on the action at Tahoe. Sure, I knew that it could not change or fix anything but I was pissed, too.


LANCER HAD BEEN reexamined and fitted with a new dressing when I returned to his hospital room. He had gotten lucky with no vital wound from the gunshot. Loss of blood had been the most dangerous effect, and Janice's quick work with a pressure bandage had undoubtedly minimized the damage. He was getting ready to go home when I found him.

He lived alone in a section convenient to the airport, near Lake Crowley. He showed me a smile and asked, "Can I get a ride home?"

I said, "Sure, I've wanted a chance to talk to you anyway. My van is over at the police station. How soon can you leave?"

"They're checking me out now. Probably five minutes."

"Hang tight," I told him. "I'll go get the van. Meet me out front."

The pilot replied, "The talk all over the hospital is about their shooting here yesterday. Lot of nice things said about you, Joe. The business at the airport last night is hardly more than a footnote around here."

I said, "That's only because they were not personally involved in that one. It's hardly a footnote, pal."

"I hear that. It'll never be a footnote to me."

I hoofed it on down to the P.D. and picked up my van from the parking lot without bothering to check in. I noticed that Chief Terry's car was not in his parking space.

Lancer was waiting for me outside the hospital entrance. "Good timing," he said.

He looked none the worse for his adventure other than a bandaged arm supported by a sling. His color was good and he looked well considering the circumstances of his night.

That changed almost immediately after we departed the hospital area. I asked him, "Did you see Janice at the hospital?"

He replied with an almost startled smile. "Well, no, I hardly expected to see her."

I said, "No, you've missed my meaning. Someone tried to kill her this morning after the incident at the plane."

The guy turned white. "That son of a bitch!" he gasped.

I said, "No, I think you have it wrong. It wasn't Sanford. Someone got to him first. He's dead."

The look on his face could only be described as mixed between a frown and a smile. "Harley's dead?" he asked.

I said, "Dead as they get, pal."

"Janice is okay?"

"She's recovering nicely. It was supposed to look like a self-inflicted drug overdose. I don't believe it was."

He said soberly, "Of course it wasn't. She doesn't do drugs. Also, Janice and I were leaving tomorrow. But of course our plans were put on hold with Martha's death."

I asked stupidly, "Leaving for where?"

"As far from that bastard as I could get her!"

Well, well. It was getting curiouser and curiouser and I could hardly wait to get the straight of that.

# CHAPTER NINETEEN

As it turned out, the pilot needed a lift only to the airport, where his car had been parked since the flight to L.A. The car seemed to be his primary concern of the moment and he insisted that he was okay to drive. He wanted to return immediately to the hospital to be with Janice. I tried to caution him about the way it might look to the police but he was adamant about being with her. I also alerted him to the fact that she had not yet been notified of her husband's death, on doctor's orders.

Lancer told me, "Sure, I understand. My only concern is for Janice, the rest of it can go to hell. I'm not worried about looking bad in any of this. I'm not sorry that Harley is dead but don't worry, I will respect Janice's feelings. As for Harley, he was the most arrogant son of a bitch I have ever known. What that woman had to put up with! He was a total bastard. I don't know how she's taken it as long as she has. He used everybody, abused everybody, even his own daughter."

I said, "Be careful how you say that, pal. A sharp prosecutor in a murder trial could give you fits with a statement like that. Especially if you've been involved with the victim's wife."

He replied, "I'd say it to anybody, now that Harley is

dead. I had nothing to do with his death and I am not afraid of making the facts known now. I was planning to leave my job even before Janice and I got together. It was primarily for her sake that I decided to stay on here as long as I could stand it."

"So how long have you been involved with Janice?"

"Long enough to be crazy in love with her."

I observed, "There's quite an age difference there."

This guy was letting it all hang out for me. "She's seven years older than me—no big deal."

I said, "I had you pegged younger than that, Tom."

"I'm forty-five. Janice married young, too young to know what she was getting into with a man like Harley Sanford. Look, the guy has been screwing around with everything in skirts as long as I've known him. I know that for a fact, at least during the time I've been flying his women around with him."

"How long has that been?"

"Nearly five years. But long before I came onto the scene, Harley's women were legend." The pilot sniffed disdainfully. "According to the stories I've heard, most of the women he was involved with until recently were prostitutes."

"Did Janice know about that?"

"Sure she knew. Harley was the kind of guy who wore his sexual indiscretions like campaign ribbons. All in all, he lived much longer than he ever should have. I have no regrets about Harley."

I said, "Don't take offense, but others could wonder if you had a powerful motive for murder, so think of this as friendly advice. With Harley dead, Janice could be worth a lot of money, which means that you could be, too, if you married her. Sorry, it's just the way cops think...and prosecutors."

He showed me a wan smile and said, "I don't give a damn what people think. I'm not interested in Janice's money."

I reminded him of our conversation aboard the plane when I tried to warn him about Sanford's problems, and added, "I told you that things could get brutal. So if there is anything you would like me to know about that, now's the time."

"I've been so torn up over Janice's problems with Harley, I guess I just haven't had a good perspective on all this. I have had a good feeling about you, though, since our conversation at Burbank, especially after you warned me about Harley. Look, I don't know from cops and, to tell you the truth, I've never thought of them as my favorite people. But I read you as a straight guy and I don't mind telling you that I've had a very insecure feeling about all this since I learned about Martha's death."

I said, "When was that?"

"It came to me out of the blue. I was down in Bishop on some business—well, okay, I was buying some things for our getaway, which was scheduled for today. My phone was ringing off the hook when I got home. It was Janice, from her car phone. She was halfway to L.A. by then and had been trying to reach me for hours. She told me about Martha."

"Quite a shock."

"To put it lightly."

"Did you know that Janice had been searching for her husband before she left for L.A.?"

"She told me, yes. She had decided to have it out with Harley before she brought Martha home, didn't want this other stuff hanging fire at such a time. I believe she felt that Harley would try to use the tragedy to keep her with him. Not that he gave a rat's ass except as his standard control mechanism."

"Sanford was good at that?"

"He was a master at that."

"So what was your scenario with Janice?"

He smiled and replied, "I wouldn't call it a scenario. We just wanted to be together, and we didn't want a lot of harassment from Harley."

"Doesn't work that way, pal, especially not with a guy like Harley Sanford in the picture. Had you and Janice discussed marriage?"

"No, mainly we just discussed divorce."

I chuckled. "First things first, huh?"

The guy had an easy smile, despite all that he had been through. He chuckled with me as he replied, "Well, sure, we talked about marriage but that seemed a long way off. I guess it's light-years now. How will we ever put it together with all this tragedy around us?"

I said, "Happens all the time. Don't focus on the tragedy. If you two are truly in love—what is that saying?— love will find a way?"

"God, I hope so," he said.

I said, softly, "Me too."

Privately, I did not give them a big chance for that. But, of course, I have been known to be wrong—about a lot of things, and especially about affairs of the heart.

As we pulled up beside his car at the airport, Lancer told me, "That business here last night—I figured Harley was behind it. Call it paranoid, I guess, but I would not have put anything past Harley Sanford. Now I have to wonder. Who do you think killed Harley, and why?"

"That's the big question of the day, pal. What seemed to be a suicide note was found on the body. How does that grab you?"

He snorted derisively. "Not that guy. All of life was an endless series of deals for Harley. He's probably right now trying to hammer out a deal in heaven—or, more likely, in hell."

"So who, would you think, wanted him dead?"

The pilot replied, "I'm much more interested in Janice's problem. You're a cop, give me a theory—who other than Harley could have wanted Janice dead?"

I told him, "The answer to that requires more than I could theorize. There are mob people hanging all over this thing. It's tied to Harley some way, but I don't have the straight of that yet."

"You'll tell me about it as soon as you work it out, won't you?"

"Bet on it. You're a sharp guy, Tom. Who wanted Harley dead?"

"Oh, there should be an endless list of candidates for that honor. You haven't been listening to me, have you? Sanford was the most 'killable' bastard I have ever known. The happiest men in town this week will be the lucky bastards who get the pleasure of serving as his pallbearers. Shit, we could sell tickets to that."

I got the message, and I had to feel that the sentiment was invoked by something more than a romantic involvement with the dead man's wife. It was scathingly obvious that this man had no admiration for his employer, in stark contrast with the initial loyalty for his boss that he had shown me, which was probably understandable in those other circumstances. After all, certain formalities go with the paycheck. I could not fault the guy for his turnaround at this time.

Look at it another way. Janice was in the catbird seat now. Technically, according to California law, she had always been coowner of the business; however, I was sure that she had never enjoyed any real power under the original status quo. Harley Sanford had obviously never been one to relinquish any power to his wife. In the present situation, Janice *was* the power.

As Lancer got out of my van and paused to turn back to thank me for the lift, I said to him, "You mentioned earlier that the news of Martha's death gave you an insecure feeling. What did you mean by that?"

He said, "Well, I guess I was just afraid that this would affect my relationship with Janice. If that makes me sound callous, I barely knew Martha. I regretted it, sure, but Janice was my major concern."

"And your plans with Janice."

"Sure, that was on my mind, I'm no saint. I was genuinely sorry about Martha but I've also been scared to death that something would get in the way of our plans."

That all seemed entirely understandable and believable. I had no feeling of guile in this guy. For his sake, and for Janice's, I hoped that it was true.

But it would be interesting to see how the "lovebirds" fared now that Harley Sanford was dead.

It was close to the noon hour when I returned to Mammoth. It was the first real chance I'd had to try to get a line on Martha's safety-deposit box.

As soon as I parked the van and stepped inside the bank there was something like a subliminal quiver that made me know I was in the right place.

It all looked so familiar, and that feeling was intensified when a bank officer at the safety-deposit counter showed me a smile and a cheery greeting. "Mr. Copp, nice to see you again. What can I do for you?"

This was the weirdest feeling, to walk in on total strangers and get that kind of recognition. Suddenly I knew this place and remembered the last time I was there. I had a flash of Martha walking beside me into the safety-deposit vault and I could even *see* the tension in her face as we were retrieving the box.

The bank official was showing me a puzzled look as I grappled with the memory. She asked me, "Are you okay?"

I tried to pass it off as I replied, "Yeah, sorry, I was thinking about something else. I need to get into my safety-deposit box."

She had me sign the card and perfunctorily verified the signature with the cards she had on file. She opened the door for me and led me back to the vault. I had no way of knowing if the key I held in my hand would open the box, but I had passed the signature test so I had to assume that it would.

It did.

I removed the box from the vault and the official escorted me to a private cubicle, where I was left alone to inspect the contents.

So far, so good. Actually, it was improper for me to access the property without notifying the bank of Martha's death, even though I was obviously a co-renter of the box. The bank official apparently had not heard about Martha's death and I saw no need to complicate things.

Things were immediately complicated enough.

I found a single three-and-a-half-inch computer floppy disk in that box. And, yeah, it would have fit perfectly inside a videotape case or small milk carton.

That was not a particularly startling discovery since I had suspected something like that after the ransacking of Arthur Douglas's apartment.

What was startling was the discovery of a thick bundle of bearer bonds. They were worth a cool million bucks.

That could be regarded as a strong motive for murder.

So maybe I had more of a credibility problem than Tom Lancer did.

# CHAPTER TWENTY

**A** BEARER BOND is in about the same league as an anonymous gift to the possessor. It belongs to whomever has the bond in hand. For the moment there, then, I was a millionaire. I will not say that I did not think of that immediately. It would not be necessary, even, to establish any right to the property; possession alone was the only criterion. Of course I had never dealt with that kind of paper and I still do not fully understand the reason for putting that much money into such an insecure arrangement. I had always assumed, in my limited understanding, that a bearer bond is most often associated with a desire to handle large sums of money in a more or less secretive manner, in order to circumvent or avoid taxes or conceal other illegal activities. But I am no financial expert, so what do I know? All I knew for sure was that I had a million bucks in my hand and that maybe it was legally mine.

So call me a jerk, and maybe I was, but I had never been overly impressed with wealth, per se. Not, anyway, enough to dirty myself to get it. That million bucks, though, had something to do with Martha's death and my reason for taking her to Los Angeles. That was not just a "feeling" but another one of those dim perceptions that had been hammering at me for the past two days.

How would Martha have come into that kind of money—legally?

Obviously, though, it had been connected to not only her murder but also to the recent intrigue in Mammoth. The life insurance money from Kaufman, according to Janice, had been only enough for Martha to set up her small business and get her going on her own. And the potential income from such a small backwoods art gallery would hardly have been enough to make her a millionaire that quickly. So where had the money come from and why had it placed her in such jeopardy?

Surely not from her own father! But maybe so. One could draw a reasonable scenario involving a guy like Harley Sanford *if the money had actually been his from the beginning* and if, for some reason, Martha had taken it and refused to return it to him.

But I had been in the bank with her when the bonds were placed in the box. I knew that was true; I had a definite memory of helping her put them there. I also knew that the bonds had been placed in the box shortly before we left for Los Angeles—which would have been very soon after the gallery burned. I could even *see* her consternation as we deposited the bonds—she was scared as hell—and I could *see* our almost panicky flight from Mammoth.

This kind of peek-a-boo memory is enough to drive a guy nuts.

I *knew*, yet "in a glass darkly," as a mystic has characterized this kind of "knowing."

I would not make a good mystic, because this shadowed reality can propel you to the very edge of insanity. When you are out there moving through that kind of darkness you can question your own perceptions at times and wonder if you will ever find the full light again.

A cop usually deals with concrete perceptions of the human reality, total logic, and hard facts. Right now I was afraid that I was dealing primarily with human emotions raging against the light. I had to discipline myself continually and wait for the light to dawn. That had never been my way. I had always been the kind of cop simply to seize the truth and try to make sense of it. That can be very difficult when you are forever staggering around half blind and half-witted—yeah, and I was feeling entirely stupid much of the time.

Thank God, it had not yet affected my trigger finger. I had the feeling, even then, that there would be plenty of fireworks ahead.


I LEFT THE bonds in the box at the bank as the safest place for them at the moment, then I took the computer diskette to a computer specialist for copying. It is amazingly fast once the technician gets a "read" on the program itself. Took this guy about twenty seconds to hand me two duplicates. The guy was good but also curious, so I elected to pass on a printout. I wanted complete privacy for that. I had no idea what information might be hidden away and I sure as hell did not feel like sharing it with a stranger.

If you are not familiar with computers, maybe this

would have little significance to you. A three-and-a-half-inch floppy diskette compresses more than a million bytes of data, which, when run through a computer, translates computer language into ordinary information according to the program originally employed. What it meant to me at the moment was nothing. I would not be able to read the copy until it was fed through a compatible computer.

The contents of a diskette are totally meaningless even to an expert until the computer itself retranslates the data into an ordinary language format. That was where I was at the moment, so I was none the wiser. I simply had preserved extra copies of the data for future use.

A small floppy such as this one could store the equivalent of several large volumes of text, so it was anybody's guess what could be concealed there. I had to feel that it was something very important and I knew that I would have to print out the information from the floppy at the earliest practical moment. I returned the original diskette to the safety-deposit box and then rented another box—in my name alone, of course—and left one of the copies in the new box. And just to circumvent any difficulty that may arise once the bank knew that Martha was dead, I also moved the bearer bonds into my own box.

I felt that my first priority was a visit to Lake Tahoe. That was my immediate destination.


LAKE TAHOE IS widely regarded as one of the loveliest lakes in the United States. It sits astride the California-

Nevada border at an elevation of more than six thousand feet, a deep-blue clear lake. The maximum depth exceeds sixteen hundred feet, ranking it among the deepest in the world. Twenty-two miles long and twelve miles wide, the state line splits the lake along a north-south axis to almost the south shore but shears off at a southeast tack a short distance above South Lake Tahoe, so that two-thirds of the lake plus the entire south shore lies within the state of California. The entire east shore of the lake and a portion of the north shore is within Nevada.

The lake has long been a popular and important resort complex for wholesome family fun and is dotted with state parks and camping facilities. Although a popular winter and summer recreational area, one of its major attractions in recent years has been the booming gambling business on the Nevada side adjoining South Lake Tahoe. The relatively few luxurious hotel casinos are closely clustered just across the Nevada line in the town of Stateline. This is nowhere in the same league as Las Vegas, but then also the natural beauty of the area far excels anything to be seen in the stark desert surroundings of Vegas.

This is of no particular moment to the inveterate gambler, since one casino seems much like another once you get inside, but it does offer a contrast to the usual atmosphere of Las Vegas, Reno, or Atlantic City. For myself, I prefer the less strident atmosphere of the High Sierra since I am no great shakes at gambling and usually regard it as an exercise in frustration.

Highway 395 takes you briefly out of California through the western tip of Nevada just south of Lake

Tahoe, on to Reno before reentering California, then through the northern part of the state and into Oregon. I jogged over to U.S. 50 just outside of Carson City, Nevada, and rolled on into Stateline at about four o'clock.

The first item of business for me was to find the wedding chapel where Martha and I were married. It was an unpretentious place near the lake. An elderly man let me in and immediately asked, "Where's the bride?"

I explained that the bride had not come with me this time and showed him the marriage certificate. "Is this one of yours?" I asked him.

He had a crackling sense of humor, showed me a droll smile as he jibed, "Did you lose her already?"

I did not want to spoil his day so I told him, "No, I'm just wondering if you remember performing the ceremony."

He studied the document with that same droll smile then replied, "Oh, it's legal, okay. Were you hoping it was not?"

"Would you believe it if I told you I'm suffering from amnesia? That's my signature, okay, but I have no memory of it. I was hoping maybe you would."

"You are serious about this?"

"Yes, sir, I am dead serious."

"What happened to your head?"

"I forgot to duck. That's why the memory loss."

The justice of the peace became entirely serious. He said, "Just a minute, please. I'll get my wife. She has a better memory for these things."

He was back within a minute, his wife in tow. She

was showing me a sympathetic smile so I knew that she was aware of the problem.

I asked her, "Do you remember me?"

She said, "Oh, yes. And such a beautiful girl."

I said, "Could I see the chapel, please?"

They took me into a small chapel in the back. Nothing elaborate, but very pretty, and I remembered this place. The scene was traumatic. I had to get out of there. I thanked the old couple and quickly let myself out. Going into that chapel had been a mistake.

I drove on into South Lake Tahoe and found the sheriff's substation. A woman on duty there recognized my name and said, "Oh, yes, Chief Terry called about you. Just a minute, please."

The guy in charge was a Sgt. Webster. He ushered me into his office and said, "I hear things have been a little hot in Mammoth."

I replied, "Too hot. L.A. is calm by comparison. How are things in Tahoe?"

He was an easy guy. "We're holding our own. Hope you're not heating things up around here the way you did in Mammoth."

I said, "Hey, I had nothing to do with it."

"You were just driving through," he said with a smile.

"The folks from your area have been behind most of the trouble down there. I was hoping that you could give me a line on some of your badasses."

"If you're talking about the guys who shot up the hospital, I don't know them. Apparently they blew through here and stole a car, but they didn't check with me first."

I chuckled and said, "I'm sure they didn't. Did you get anything on their movements here?"

"Yeah, we made them at the airport. Apparently they had come in from back East by way of San Francisco. These guys were connected. It was a contract job, I'm sure of that."

"Who, would you think, was sponsoring them?"

"At this stage, it's anybody's guess."

I said, "How about the guys who ripped off the military Jeep in Nevada? Any score on those two?"

He showed me a sober smile. "The Nevada authorities are putting together a package on them. At first glance, they were for sale to anybody with a few bucks. Why Mammoth?"

I said, "Looks like it's all somehow involved with Harley Sanford's problems. John Terry told you that Sanford was found dead in Mammoth this morning?"

"Yeah. Sanford is a big man around here but he's strictly a small fish in a large pond. Hell, he wouldn't be worth much cut down to his own size. I suspect that's exactly what's been behind all this. He just got too big for his pants."

I said, "Maybe so. What can you tell me about a couple of small-time hoods who've been playing games for Sanford? According to the rap sheets that Terry gave me, Sammy and Clifford spend a lot of time up here. What do you know about these guys?"

"Yeah, they're small-time, go-fer jobs for Sanford. For some reason, he seemed to enjoy having punks like these on his payroll, but I don't know how involved they may have been."

"Were they involved with his casino?"

"Like I said, go-fers; they hung around a lot but I never found them with anything dirty on this side of the border." Webster pulled a sheath of paper from his drawer and said, "I thought you'd never ask." He passed the file on to me. "This turned up just a few hours ago."

Sammy and Clifford were dead, victims of a mysterious "boating accident."

I said, "How convenient."

"Freak accident. It says that they fell from the boat and it went on without them. Apparently neither man could swim. The boat was run ashore on the west side."

I said, "If you can believe that..."

Webster snickered. "One way is as good as another, I guess."

"Death by drowning?"

"That's the tentative finding. There were bruises on both bodies."

"No witnesses?"

"Oh, yeah, some fishermen saw the boat running wild and the two men thrashing around in the water. Took some hours for the divers to find the bodies. This is a very deep lake, you know."

I said, "Well, those guys had been trying to buy into something like that for a long time, I guess. I don't care what it might look like, those guys were snuffed."

Webster snorted. "Takes no genius to figure that out."

I stood up and grasped his hand. "Thanks for the briefing. I know you're a busy man. I want to take a look at the casino."

He walked me outside and told me, "Don't be a stranger. Stop by anytime."

That was pleasant enough.

Except that the dark shadow of death seemed to be following me around, even into the depths of Lake Tahoe.

I was getting a bellyful of this stuff.

And it was not done yet.

# CHAPTER TWENTY-ONE

**I**F IT SOUNDS as though I were merely stumbling around in the dark here, let me remind you that is exactly what I had been doing for days, but I cannot blame all of my difficulties on my head trauma. The events of the past couple of days would have been bewildering enough even had I been fully in control of my head. It did seem, however, that the deeper I got into this case the better my memory became. The visit at the wedding chapel, though painful, had furthered to some extent my sense of reality concerning the entire experience. So I was really looking forward to a bit more "shock treatment" as I moved closer toward the truth about Martha.

I drove past her father's casino and wanted an inside look at that place, but that could wait. Terry had given me a line on the Sanford home, which was nearby, and I wanted to check that out first.

It turned out to be a rather modest lakeside home, by Sanford's standards, with the yard a bit neglected and the house exterior suffering from inattention.

I did not have any trouble getting inside. French doors on the lakeside appeared to have been broken into recently and hastily patched with duct tape. I removed the tape and the glass, reached through, easily found the lock, and just walked right in.

It was a nice-enough house, sure, but nothing to write up in House and Garden.

Especially not this particular house.

There was a horrible odor, one I had experienced many times in the past.

I discovered a dead woman in the bedroom.

She had been there long enough for the body to have begun decomposing—and the odor in there was over-powering.

She was naked, face-up on the bed, dead of apparent gunshot wounds.

Her clothing was folded neatly atop the dresser. A purse contained ten crisp twenty-dollar bills, an un-opened package of cigarettes, various other odds and ends, a small cosmetic bag, and a wallet with a Nevada driver's license. The photo on the license was close enough and her date of birth indicated that she was twenty-five years old, residence Carson City, Nevada. The name was given as Vicki Lynn Douglas!

It is not that uncommon a name, but I almost twitched when I read it; there had to be a connection here to Arthur Douglas. It had been a large group of the "Doug-las clan" in the waiting room at the hospital in Mam-moth—and Carson City is not far removed.

I had to get out of there for some fresh air. I took the driver's license with me to the van and snapped a close-up shot of it with my Polaroid. Then I returned the document to the dead girl's wallet.

I poked around briefly inside the house but found no

further interest there. This house had none of the charm
or grace of the Sanford home at Mammoth; there was
no family warmth here. Obviously it had been used primarily as a vacation residence and not even that to any
extent during recent years.

A boat slip on the water was also showing signs of
disuse and neglect. I wondered if this place had figured
during happier times when Martha, George Kaufman,
Arthur Douglas, and Cindy Morgan had posed for the
photo I had earlier found in the wreckage of Douglas's
apartment in Mammoth.

I just wanted to get out of there as quickly as possible.
I called the Nevada Sheriff's Department and went out-
side to wait for their arrival. I had done all I could do.
Now it was a job for the coroner.


TWO OFFICERS FROM the Nevada Sheriff's Department
were on the scene within minutes after my call. These
guys were sharp and knew exactly how to handle this
kind of investigation, so I did not accompany them inside the house. That was no worry, because they were
not anxious to dally around in there any more than I
had been. My name meant nothing to them and they
were even less impressed with my P.I. badge, but they
were courteous and friendly.

They did know of Harley Sanford, and it would have
disappointed me if they had not. These Nevada cops
have some kind of radar concerning known casino operators. They'd even had this home on some sort of
check list and one of them made a reference to the APB

out of Mammoth. Of course they asked me repeatedly about my knowledge of the victim and her relationship with Sanford.

I saw no need at this time to mention my suspicion that this dead girl could be a relative of the cop who had been shot in Mammoth, Arthur Douglas, but I did consider it prudent to mention the recent string of violence; I did have to explain why I was in the area and why I had entered the house.

I recited the facts as I knew them, but only the facts without embellishment. They asked me about the two victims who had been found in the lake earlier that day. I explained that I had learned of that just a few minutes earlier from the California authorities and they did not question me further about that incident. I could tell that they were interested, however.

One of the cops was on his radio even as I spoke. I suspected that the Nevada authorities were checking out my story because the guy kept glancing my way the whole time he was on the radio.

It took me an hour to get clear of there. The cops offered me nothing about the dead girl except to hint that she had been known in the area and I overheard one of them suggest to the other that the victim was "an unlucky hooker."

I was still mulling that possibility and trying to get on my way when another Nevada cop rolled in and stepped out of his vehicle to show me interested attention. He looked vaguely familiar. The name on his chest was Miller and I divined from his identification that he was a watch commander or its equal in this neck of the woods. He greeted me in a familiar way and asked, "What are you into this time, Joe?"

It can be annoying as hell to be constantly in one identity crisis after another, unable to focus in on events that should be strongly in the mind, especially at a time like this. But I did not get a chance to even try to focus on this guy. His radio began squawking and he had to make a dash for his car. "Sorry," he yelled at me over his shoulder. "Gotta run!" From the gist of what I heard on his radio, an ambulance was responding to an auto accident uplake somewhere. He showed me an amiable smile as he peeled out of there.

That was okay with me. I was not feeling exactly sociable at the moment, anyway. I was still struggling with the riddle of Vicki Douglas.

If Tom Lancer had given me the straight on Harley Sanford, then it was not exactly a surprising revelation that this latest victim had spent time in the Sanford house. But had he killed her there?—and if so, why in God's name had he simply walked away and left the body in his own bed?

If Sanford had not killed her, who had?—and why? This victim had been dead since sometime before the recent events in Mammoth. From the condition of the body, it was even conceivable that she could have died at about the same time that Martha died—or even earlier.

It was going to be interesting to see the coroner's report on this one.

It would be even more interesting if Vicki Douglas had a definite family connection with the wounded officer in Mammoth and if "an unlucky hooker" in Tahoe was somehow involved in the wave of intrigue stretching from Los Angeles to Mammoth and beyond.

I was betting that she was.

Something deep inside of me was crying out that she was.

But how?

I DROVE A short distance back to "Sanford's Tahoe," the casino that bore his name although he was only one of several owners. This was no "Caesar's Palace" by any stretch of the imagination, but it was nice enough, large enough, and no doubt lucrative in any way that really counts for a casino operator.

According to Nevada law, only a small percentage of casino gambling profits may be retained by the casinos. Theoretically, at least, the lion's share of gambling earnings must be returned as winnings, so the margin of profit for the operator should be better when nongambling expenses are minimized. Since the glitzy casinos in Las Vegas and elsewhere ordinarily operate at practically giveaway prices for rooms, food, and beverages, the profit margins for the small-time casino operators are no doubt considerably higher than those who feel obliged to encourage the gambling public with expensive perks.

This one had a small lounge and only a "snack bar" to divert attention from the main business at hand, gambling—no rooms, no entertainment, no "perks" that I could discern—plenty of slot machines, several crap tables, a number of blackjack tables, poker tables, even a baccarat room and the ever-present keno action.

Business was good, for early evening. The tables were active and the slots were getting heavy play if the noise in there could be a good indication—bells ringing and lights flashing to keep the players excited and hopeful.

I made my way up a wide flight of stairs to the casino office and had to run a gauntlet of wary security officers who where manning the ramparts above the casino floor. The casino boss was a studious-looking guy of about fifty with wire-framed glasses and a harried expression. He came forward to greet me in the outer office after I flashed my badge at a young woman inside who had leapt to the conclusion that I was a police detective.

I did not even have to show the badge a second time. The casino boss showed me interested attention and ushered me into his office. He was a busy man, so I got right to the point. "Harley Sanford was killed this morning," I told him.

"My *God!*" he cried.

I said, "Shocking, yeah. He was shot."

"I can't *believe* this!"

"Believe it," I suggested. "I am investigating his death. Can you think of anyone who may have wanted him dead?"

The guy was still bowled over by the information. "Not Mr. Sanford, no, my God! Wonderful man, I can't believe it!"

I told him, "I've never heard him described as a wonderful man. From what I've heard, people have been standing in line for years to put him away."

"Oh, no, I don't think that's true. He was a hard business man, sure, but not..."

"There's a theory that he might have killed himself. What would you think of that?"

"I can't believe that, either. This is just..."

"Do you know Mrs. Sanford?"

"I haven't seen her for a couple of years, uh..."

"Since Kaufman died?"

"Come to think of it, I guess not since then."

"Did you know Kaufman?"

"Sure. He was the controller here."

"Did you know Martha?"

"Sure, I know Martha."

I told him, "No, you have that in the wrong tense. Martha was murdered more than a week ago in Los Angeles."

The guy's eyes were popping through the wire rims. He was overloading on this information. He stood up and walked around the office before again taking his chair, and the eyes were moist as he said, "God, I can't believe this. Martha was a wonderful girl. Why would anyone...?"

He was one of those people who seldom complete a statement. I told him, "Another girl was found dead a short while ago here in Tahoe." I showed him the Polaroid of the Douglas girl's driver's license. "Do you know this victim?"

He inspected the snapshot closely and lingered for a moment on the DMV photo. "Yes, I know this woman. She comes in here a lot."

I asked, "Have you ever seen her in the presence of Harley Sanford?"

The casino boss was beginning to get his wits about him. He gave me a wary look and replied, "I couldn't swear that I have. A lot of women come in here."

"In Sanford's company?"

"I really couldn't say."

"Sure you could. Don't get delicate with me, pal. This is important. The man is dead, the girl is dead. Did Sanford know her?"

The casino boss's gaze swerved aside as he replied in a barely audible voice, "Yes, he knew her."

"He knew her very well, didn't he?"

"Yes."

"That's better. When did you last see her?"

"Maybe a couple of weeks ago."

"With Sanford?"

"Yes."

"Do you know her connection to Arthur Douglas?"

"That's the cop that works down in Mammoth?"

"That's the one."

"I believe they're cousins."

I said, "Great. Did you know that Arthur Douglas was shot and nearly killed in Mammoth yesterday?"

"God, no! Douglas used to come up to the Sanford home a lot. He and Martha went to school together in Mammoth. So who went gunning for Arthur?"

I told him, "That is under investigation. How well do you know Mrs. Sanford?"

"Hardly at all. She's a wonderful woman but she never spent much time with the business."

"How much time have you spent with the Sanfords?"

"I think," the casino boss said warily, "I should let the attorneys know what's going on before I say any more. You understand. I'm a hired hand here. Anything involving the owners . . . "

I said, "You've had another tragedy here today. Two of your employees were found dead in the lake this morning. Were you notified of that?"

But our "rapport" had been broken. The casino boss had lost patience with this line of questioning. He replied, rather shortly, "Sam Mescina and Cliff Blandino? They were not employees in the usual sense."

"In what sense were they?"

"I'm afraid I don't understand."

"Of course you do. They worked for Harley Sanford, didn't they?"

"Well, they were not on the casino payroll."

"But you'd heard of their accident?"

"Yes."

I said, "That's all?—they were not wonderful men and you simply can't believe that they're dead?"

"I don't know what you expect me to say. I hardly knew these guys. They hung around the casino a lot, and of course I knew that Mr. Sanford sometimes employed them, but not in connection with the casino."

"Sammy and Clifford were small-time hoods with criminal records going back for years. Sanford was not worried about associating with people like these?"

"Mr. Sanford could be very generous and understanding."

I said, "Bullshit."

He replied, "I don't have to take that from you, Mr. Copp. Is there anything else I can do for you?"

I had overstayed my welcome. Actually, I had gotten away with much more than I had thought I would.

I stood up and said, "Thanks for your cooperation." The relief was evident in the casino boss's eyes. He thought he was home free but I was not done with him yet. He walked me to the door, and as I turned back to shake his hand I asked him, "What exactly does a controller do in a place like this?"

He replied, breathing easier now, "It's sort of like the chief accountant. It's an important job, keeps the business matters straight with the IRS and all that."

"So George Kaufman was in a critical post."

"Oh, sure. George was plenty sharp, too."

"Sanford was the principal partner?"

"Oh, yes, Mr. Sanford was the controlling owner."

"How was Martha involved?"

That one startled him. He replied, "Martha was never involved as far as I knew."

"And her husband was simply an employee?"

"Well, yes, but it can never hurt to marry the boss's daughter. That fellow really screwed up, didn't he? If he had played his cards right, maybe he would have owned all of this one day."

"What killed the marriage?"

The guy was trying to show that he was being friendly. He dropped his voice and gave me a knowing look as he replied, "Well, he preferred boys, you know."

No, of course, I had not known that until maybe this very moment—but a fragment of memory was zinging me as I walked out of there, something Martha had told me while we were honeymooning. And, yes, I suspected that I had known that the guy was gay.

But what could that have brought to the understanding of things known?

Unless, maybe, Harley Sanford had murdered his own son-in-law. It would not be unbelievable.

# CHAPTER TWENTY-TWO

**H**ARLEY SANFORD COULD have been the kind of man who would regard it as a personal affront to learn that his daughter's husband was homosexual, even as heinous if the "gender problem" had been concealed before the marriage. A "self-made man" such as Sanford could regard the anomaly as the worst treachery. I could even envision a scenario in which the offended father would be angry enough to kill. So it was not too far a reach, for me, to wonder if Sanford had been directly responsible for his son-in-law's death. I would want to look into the investigation of Kaufman's "accident" by the local authorities.

I was shooting in the dark, sure, but I had been *living* in the dark since I awoke in a hospital room three days earlier, so what was new?

I found Vicki Douglas's residence in one of the more modest neighborhoods on the outskirts of Carson City. A woman of about fifty answered my ring at the door. Evidently she had already been notified of her daughter's death. She had been weeping and wore that stunned expression that is so characteristic of the families of murder victims. Has something to do with the realization of death out of its place and time—a needless, stupid, senseless death, as others have characterized the experience.

I had seen plenty enough of that sort of thing these past two days, so I could sympathize with this mother's trauma. She was a nice lady, probably never hurt another creature in all her life, and simply could not understand how something like this could happen.

She told me that the police had already been there and she had told them everything she knew but she was anxious to help in any way she could. She invited me in for "a refreshment," which I declined, but I did step inside just to get a flavor of the place. It was small and rather bare but immaculate and homey.

Vicki still lived there, yes, but had been spending a lot of time away from home for the past year. She sort of "came and went" but "that was okay" because she knew that this was not "too eventful a life" for a young girl.

I asked about Vicki's friends and family, in particular her connection to Arthur Douglas.

"Arthur is my late husband's nephew," she replied. "He's a policeman in Mammoth."

"So you know about his recent problem in Mammoth?"

"You mean the shooting, yes."

I said, "Doesn't it seem to you that there is a connection between the problem in Mammoth and your daughter's death?"

She gave me a blank look. "How could it be connected?"

I told her, "Seems that way to me. How well do you know the Sanford family?"

She sniffed at the mention of that name and said, "They are not nice people."

"None of them?" I asked.

"Not one of them," she replied firmly.

"Do you know Mrs. Sanford?"

"Only to see flashing around the lakeside in a big car. No, I don't know any of them."

"Not Mr. Sanford?"

"No."

"Hadn't Vicki been working for Mr. Sanford?"

"I told her she shouldn't."

"But was she?"

"I don't know. He called her a lot. She said he wanted her to work in his casino."

"That shouldn't be a bad job."

She said, "Then obviously you don't know that man."

"But neither do you," I reminded her.

"I know enough," she said, and that seemed to close the subject in her mind.

She did, however, invite me to look at her daughter's room.

"The other officer saw everything there is to see, but you're welcome to look again."

I have no idea what the "other officer" saw or did not see in that room because "seeing" is often a totally subjective experience.

What I saw was a small, fairly recent photo of Vicki Douglas with Janice Sanford in a rather intimate shot with two other men, neither of whom was Harley Sanford. These people were barely dressed but I could not determine if they were in or near the water—perhaps they were in swim attire but this angle did not look that innocent.

One of the men was Chief Pilot Tom Lancer.

The other was my old pal from Mammoth, Police Chief John Terry.

But what did it mean? It could mean anything or nothing... and I was not betting on "nothing."


I WAS SUDDENLY feeling anxious about Janice Sanford and knew that I wanted to get back to Mammoth without delay, although I had not learned a hell of a lot at Tahoe, not in any positive sense. I found myself wishing I had not come, and even for a moment I entertained the idea of simply placing all the dead at final rest and closing the door on the whole thing. It was getting uglier and more disturbing with every new development, and I think maybe I was afraid of what even more shocking revelations might still be awaiting me.

But I could not simply bail out. Too many people were now at the mercy of this runaway steed called death, so I was in for the course, whatever that may be.

I stopped at a convenience store beside the highway off U.S. 395 to check in with Chief Terry at Mammoth. I had decided that there would be nothing to gain by looking into the two-year-old police investigation of the death of George Kaufman. I was feeling a more immediate agitation now. Terry leaped at my call the moment the switchboard put me through.

He tensely asked me, "Where are you, bud?"

"Just out of Carson City. What's the status on Janice Sanford?"

"Glad you asked. She checked herself out of the hospital about six o'clock. I haven't been able to contact her at home. The phone service is back on but she isn't responding. I've even driven by a couple of times. I'm really concerned."

"You ought to be. I found three more victims here at Tahoe."

He cussed beneath his breath. "I heard about Sammy and Clifford. The Sheriff's Department at Tahoe gave me a call."

"When did you last see those two?"

"I guess it was during the rhubarb at Martha's gallery when you tossed their butts outside."

"And you told me recently that you thought they had returned to L.A."

"So I was wrong about that. You knew that. You told me that you discovered them looting Martha's condo your first day back in town. So what are you getting at?"

I said, "You didn't mention that they usually hung out at Sanford's casino in Tahoe."

"Maybe not, but I recall telling you about a conversation I'd had with the sheriff's people up there. So what?"

I said, "So, if these were just a couple of small-time hoods, who had such a hard-on for these guys?"

"According to the information I was given, they had a boating accident."

"Sure, and you can follow the 'yellow brick road' all around the area if you'd like to. Those guys had become an embarrassment to someone. Their sponsor, Sanford, was already out of the picture when they died. Or maybe all three were killed at about the same time, but in different cities, miles apart. You can't miss the 'coincidence' of all these people on a hit list at roughly the same time, and you have to include Janice in that. They're all connected."

Terry said gruffly, "Sure, I've caught that. But you mentioned three new victims at Tahoe. Who the hell else?"

I gave it to him cold. "Vicki Douglas. I think you knew the lady."

There was a long silence at the other end before he recovered to say, "Jesus! When?"

"If you mean when did I find her, that was just a few hours ago. But she had been dead for a long time, I'm guessing maybe two weeks. It will take a coroner's expertise to determine the time and cause of death. I'm guessing gunshot but the body is in a fairly bad state of decomposition."

This news intensified Terry's discomfort. Maybe he was looking at a vision of the close call by Janice Sanford that very day. He said, angrily, "Enough of this shit!"

I replied, "Tell me about it. I can't even keep count now."

"Where did the girl die?"

"Get ready for this one, pal. She died in Harley Sanford's bed at Lake Tahoe."

He cussed some more, then said, "I knew that kid. She was Art's cousin."

"I heard. Also heard one of the Nevada cops refer to her as a hooker. True?"

"How the hell would I know? To some of these cops,

every woman is a hooker, even their own wives. So what if she was?"

I said, "Hey, don't unload on me, pal. I was just telling it like I got it. Apparently the girl had been involved in the past with Harley Sanford, spent a lot of time in his casino. I also found a picture of her at her mother's home. You knew her, too, John."

"So string me up. I've known several people who have not survived involvement with that guy. So what are you saying?"

I said, "Testy, testy. It's okay, so am I. This thing is getting to me, too, John. I'm about ready to hang it all up."

"Maybe you should. I have some information for you, too. Two of your pals from the big city blew in here about five o'clock. They're hot for your body. You didn't hear this from me, of course, but they brought warrants with them."

"I didn't hear that, no. Andrews and Zambrano?"

"Yeah. They're putting on the feed bag right now at The Chart House. I told them you'd gone up to Tahoe for a few days. Maybe you shouldn't make a liar of me."

"Dammit, that's going to complicate things. I would rather take myself in, but not before this thing unravels a bit."

"Well, you know, I have very little latitude here. None at all, in fact. But if you're telling me that you're still at Tahoe, I hear you, and it's my duty to pass that info along."

"Let's leave it that way, then."

"You've got it, bud. Look for company as soon as they hit your area—if you're still there."

I said, "Yeah, thanks, I have that. Look for Janice at Lancer's place."

"You know something I don't?"

"I'm just saying that you should look for her at Lancer's."

"I read that. Thanks. You know, of course, that you and I can't be talking this way until you've resolved your misunderstandings in L.A."

I told him, "Yeah, thanks, I understand. Tell Andrews and Zambrano that I called you. Cover yourself."

I knew and he knew that he had to do exactly that. I also knew, though, that this guy would never just hang me out to dry.

I hoped that the two L.A. cops would be well on their way to Tahoe before I got to Mammoth.

I also knew that no one could cover my ass on this thing forever.

I had to break this case. I had to break it quickly and decisively.

Janice Sanford's fate could be in the balance. Mine, too.

# CHAPTER TWENTY-THREE

SOME OF THE sharpest cops on the continent were apparently right now building a shroud for Joe Copp, and maybe the shroud would not wait for my memory to reassert itself.

It would be only a matter of time, I knew, before these people would be all over my butt—and properly so, I have to say. They had my own gun as the murder weapon that blew Martha apart and a suspect whose only "defense" was a schmaltzy story about "amnesia." I would not have bought that one myself, coming from someone else. So I knew what these guys were thinking and I could not even blame them. So I was their chief suspect in what had now developed into a string of murders. The mystery to me, of the moment, was why John Terry was still speaking to me.

Those considerations were driving me all the way back to Mammoth. I had to get a handle on this thing and I had to get it damned quick. But I was being driven into a corner that was pulling me tighter and tighter; so how much play did I have left?

I was cut off now, even, from my access to Terry. I could not and would not expect him to continue to shelter me from the warrants out of Los Angeles. And, yes,

I was definitely feeling like a hunted fugitive—which, to my dismay, was exactly the situation.

So to hell with it. More and more, it was beginning to appear to me that Janice Sanford was in much greater jeopardy than I was, and that was the problem I had to focus on.

Problem was, I could not find Janice Sanford—not at the Sanford home and not with Tom Lancer. I suspected—no, I hoped—that Lancer had taken her into hiding somewhere.

I returned to the Sanford house and jimmied a lock to get inside.

Another déjà vu.

The whole place was a disaster area. This time, though, I had at least an inkling of what this string of burglaries was about.

Each of them, I would have taken book on it, was about a million bucks in bearer bonds. That was a good enough theory to begin with, anyway.

I wondered if the house had been in that shape before Janice returned home from the hospital—and if that was *why* Lancer had spirited her away. Or maybe he had simply taken her to a hotel as a refuge from the mess.

So I returned to Lancer's place and broke into that one, too. Again, someone had been ahead of me but much neater than the usual routine. Even so, they had been determined as hell to get to those bonds, or whatever. I was betting on the bonds, but what the hell did I know? They could have been looking for anything, and I was leaving all options open.

But where did that leave me?

With a sinking gut, that's where it left me.

It was now closing on eleven P.M. I was flailing around, and I knew it, when I drove into town and parked at the hotel.

There was a stranger at the front desk, a guy of about forty. "I was hoping to find Marie on duty," I told him.

He said, "Check the coffee shop, sir."

I did, and I scored.

Very interesting woman.

There is something about a mature woman that often intrigues me. A police-department shrink once suggested to me that it had something to do with my mother, as though it were some sort of wish fulfillment.

I don't know about that part of it, but my mother did abandon me at a tender age; all I know for sure is that I have always felt comfortable with women older than me. Don't try to develop anything Freudian about this. I like women, period, and I don't stop liking them, whether or not they've aged a bit.

Marie came at me like a long-lost friend. She cried, "Boy, am I glad to see you. I've been wanting to talk to someone about Cindy Morgan but I guess I'm a little intimidated by cops."

I joined her at the table and told her, "Don't feel bad about it; cops intimidate me, too."

She smiled and said, "Takes one to know one, doesn't it. I'm not afraid of you, though, Joe. Did you come looking for me?"

"Maybe I picked up your vibes," I replied. "Yeah, I came looking for you. You have something to tell me about Cindy?"

She really was quite attractive, obviously intelligent and downright flirty. She leaned closer and with a seductive air said, "Is this place okay for you?"

I asked, "Did you have something else in mind?"

"Can't get much privacy here," she replied soberly.

I did not know why not; we were the only ones in the whole place except for a cook and a waitress, both half asleep in the back. I told her, with a joking leer, "You're scaring the hell out of me, Marie. Let's just keep it right here. What else is on your mind?"

"Scaredy-cat. You need some attention to your head injury. And whatever else needs attention. Have you eaten?"

I said, "I grabbed a hamburger a while ago. Where do you live?"

"I have an apartment right here at the hotel. Nice apartment. Do you have a place to stay tonight?"

"Now that you mention it, I guess I don't."

"You do now, if you want it."

I said, "Well, we do need a quiet place to talk. It's too damned noisy in here."

She had a great sense of humor. That observation was as funny to her as it was to me. "So let's get out of here," she giggled.

So we got out of there. But it took us a while to get back to the point of our discussion. Hell, it took quite a while. And I remembered, then, what it was about older women that charmed me so.

SHE GAVE ME attention, all right—from the top of my head to the tip of my toes. And she had been right, I really needed that—to block out the shocking reality that had been pummeling me these past two days—and

I needed sanctuary, at least for a moment.

Some may feel that I am an insensitive, sexist lout after all this talk about my sense of tragedy over the death of Martha. I can only say that it had been a furious and even sometimes numbing experience from almost the beginning, and of course I only now and then had a foggy recall of Martha. I needed Marie—thank God for her and the respite that she provided me during a difficult time.

Besides that, it was beautiful and she was beautiful. Such *fire* in that woman—and, yes, there will always be a special place in my heart for her.

It was a brief respite, however. One of Terry's people must have spotted me going in—or maybe they had spotted my van outside and someone put the pieces together, whatever, but Chief Terry was at Marie's door at one o'clock.

I heard him apologizing for the intrusion as she answered his soft knock at the door. She did not seem the least flustered or embarrassed—but definitely unhappy with the interruption—as she announced his presence while skipping through to the privacy of her bathroom.

This was the type of accommodation supplied to top management personnel in the hotel trade. It was actually a suite of rooms, quite homey and comfortable with all the normal trappings of residential needs.

There was an entirely serviceable kitchen area, large bath with shower, expensive television with VCR and cable hookups, spacious living room with a sun deck, and a master bedroom suite with a king bed.

I slipped on my pants and went to the door to meet the chief outside. He said, "Sorry if I broke up anything here, bud, but I thought you would want to know about this."

I replied, "It's okay. What's up?"

"Your pals from L.A. got blown away a few minutes ago."

I guess I just stared at him stupidly for a moment before I inquired, "Where was this—Tahoe?"

"No, they never got to Tahoe. Someone blew them off the highway north of Lee Vining. I'm going to run up there. Would you like to go with me?"

"Give me a minute," I told him.

"Make it quick. I'll be waiting in the car."

Marie came out of the bathroom the minute I closed the door and grabbed for my clothes. "Is the party over?" she asked.

"For now, I'm afraid so." I struggled into my clothes as I reminded her, "There was something you wanted to tell me about Cindy Morgan."

"I guess it can wait," she replied.

I said, "No, let's have it."

"I just wanted you to know that Cindy was planning on leaving. Today was to have been her last day on the job. She and Harley Sanford were going away together."

"How do you know that?"

She scooped a small package from a bedside table. "She was in such a state the day she died, she left this behind in her drawer at the front desk."

There were two airline tickets in that package, made out to Mr. and Mrs. Harley Sanford, and the destination was San Juan, Puerto Rico. They were one-way tickets.

"They were leaving Saturday," Marie told me. "And it looks like they were not planning on coming back."

I said, "That's the way it looks, yeah, but how do you know that Cindy had not merely picked up those tickets for the Sanfords?"

"Because I know that one of these tickets was for Cindy. She had been excited for a week and she even quit her job. I know it belonged to her."

I thanked her and added, "Hang on to these tickets until I get back. They could be very important. Good work. I'll discuss this with you later."

"So you're coming back?"

"Sure, soon as I can. But it's police business so . . ." I kissed her warmly and told her, "Just don't wait up for me."

Terry was waiting in the squad car just outside the lobby entrance. He was wheeling it even as I was closing my door. He said, as we hurtled onto the street, "Hope I didn't cramp your style there, bud, but I figured you would want to be in on this."

"Thanks, yes, I appreciate it. Hope this doesn't mean that I'm a suspect."

"This is no Toonerville police force here, you know. We've known your movements from the minute you hit our city limits." He showed me a droll smile without missing a beat on the rapidly accelerating police car. "You and Marie—I would never have suspected it."

I said, "Why not? Attractive woman. They don't all have to be twenty and dumb."

He was enjoying this. "My sentiments exactly, but still . . ."

"Still nothing," I retorted. "She's a lot of woman. And, incidentally, she has some information that she's holding for you."

"What's that?"

"It seems that Harley and Cindy Morgan were planning on running away together. At least, it looks that way to me. Cindy gave notice and quit her job last week. She and Harley had booked flight to Puerto Rico for this weekend—one-way tickets."

The chief almost lost a beat with his car. "I would have to question that information," he said stiffly. "He couldn't just—well, maybe he could, but not that way. Harley had too much at stake here, a hell of a business empire. I could buy Puerto Rico for a few days, sure, but not forever."

I said, "Maybe not, but maybe his 'empire' was not as stable as one might think. Maybe he needed an escape and he took it. And maybe that's why the whole kingdom seems to be falling apart around him."

The Chief sighed. "Well, I don't know. Everything seemed to be just beautiful a mere week ago."

"Maybe it was and maybe it wasn't. The whole works was falling apart, it seems, as of about the time George Kaufman died." The Chief shot me a disturbed glance as I continued. "So okay, this is pure theory, but I'm picking up the long-distance marks on this tragedy from a long way back."

"So you're a psychic, now."

"Doesn't take a psychic to read these signs, pal," I said. "The whole thing was going rotten. I don't know from what, exactly, or from who, but this family was going into self-destruct long before I first encountered it. Why didn't you tell me that something had been going on between you and Janice Sanford?"

"Don't you mean Martha? I told you about that."

"No, I meant Janice."

"Hold it there, bud. You're shooting from the hip again."

I said, "No, I'm talking reality here, pal. I saw a picture of you and Janice at Tahoe. Harley wasn't in it and I just cannot picture him behind the camera. Don't give me any crap about the age difference. Janice Sanford is a beautiful woman and you aren't exactly a kid yourself. So when are you going to level with me?"

He stomped the brakes and screeched to a halt on a shoulder of the road just outside of town, took a long, hard look at me, and then asked, "Am I going to have to kick the shit out of you, bud, gimpy head and all?"

I grinned and said, "God, I hope not."

He chuckled and I chuckled, then we started off again. This guy had a very endearing and entirely credible way about him.

Again, though, I was hoping that I was not wrong about this guy.

# CHAPTER TWENTY-FOUR

SOMEONE HAD PLANNED this one to a close count. The L.A. County unmarked sheriff's car had apparently been midway through a curve along the divided highway section of Conway Summit, a long grade pulling to above 8,000 feet at the crest, when they were hit.

This can be a somewhat desolate drive during late night when highway traffic is at a minimum. The small town of Lee Vining, just south of the pull toward the summit, is the last town encountered until reaching Bridgeport, about twenty-five miles to the north. Just east of Lee Vining stands the eerie, almost moonscape desolation of Mono Lake, an ancient sea nearly 700,000 years old and regarded as one of the oldest lakes in North America, surrounded by volcanic craters still regarded as seismically active today.

You could read the markings on this hit almost as though it were a movie script. It had come about with the same deadly accuracy and timing as the hit on Arthur Douglas in Mammoth. The shooter had known the locale and conditions best favorable to his intentions. Both men had been shot in the head by powerful bullets that probably had been wielded by a high-powered rifle or maybe a shotgun using deer slugs. They probably did not know what hit them.

The vehicle had traveled only a brief distance before swerving across the lanes and then back to bury itself, wheels down, against the surrounding mountainside. There were no witnesses on the scene. The vehicle had been spotted by a trucker who had called it in on his citizen's band radio without remaining on the scene; presumably he had not witnessed the attack and knew only that a car had gone off the road.

The state police were on the scene as well as two sheriff's units. We arrived at about the same time as the coroner's vehicle from Bridgeport. The police on the scene had made only a cursory examination of the bodies to identify them and to confirm that they were beyond help. Their wounds were massive and death no doubt instant. The investigating officers were nervous and obviously still a bit spooked by the realization that it could come to any of them at any time, with no more warning than these two had had.

I had known these victims, although one of them very briefly, so I guess I was a bit more angry than anything else. It always hits a bit close to home when the victim is a fellow officer. That is not because the death of a cop is more important than other deaths. It is because there is more a sense of personal identification with the victim, even a stranger.

In this case, I knew these guys personally, so the sense of loss was more immediate. Making it even worse, it was a cold ambush. There was no other way to look at it. The marks were all there, and so obvious. The shooter or shooters had followed the vehicle and then ran on ahead for a distance before picking their spot, quickly scrambling into position alongside the road, and then coolly lying in wait. That was the way I read it.

Andrews and Zambrano had been shot through the right window of their moving vehicle—two sudden blasts from a high-powered rifle, and it was as quick as that.

But why?

Why them?

One of the shooters had followed them on foot while their shattered vehicle careened along the death path. The cops on the scene already had all the marks on that. A clear set of footprints, right foot only, began from a fresh tar spot beside the road some fifty yards behind the wrecked vehicle, went toward the vehicle and then returned.

Someone had been as cool as ice and implacable in the determination to take something from that vehicle. They had been fearless enough, or desperate enough, to stay with it, risking imminent discovery while ripping everything out of the trunk and glove compartment in a frenzied search along a public highway.

What the hell could Andrews and Zambrano have found in Mammoth of sufficient importance to have marked them for death on a lonely country highway? Couldn't have been the bonds or anything else that I could fathom—but, what the hell, it was just as expert and daring as the other shootings had been. And this gave me a little quiver reaching all the way back to L.A. and my own shooting. Not that I had more than a quiver, but in some subliminal corner of my mind, I felt that it must have happened almost exactly this way.

So what the hell did it mean? What did it *mean?*

I asked Chief Terry, "What were these guys looking for in town?"

He growled, "Beats me, bud." He was madder'n hell. "But if I find it..."

I said, "You can't miss the pattern here."

"I can't? Just watch my lips. I can't even *find* it. This is insanity."

"You know better than that."

"Do I? Okay—sure—I know that. And I knew that Andrews and Zambrano had been nosing around in Mammoth. Ostensibly they were here to pick you up. But they were doing more than that."

"So what were they doing?"

"They were investigating the death of Martha Kaufman."

"But they already had their suspect."

"I'm not so sure of that."

"What are you saying?"

He gave me a wry smile. "These guys didn't want you. They could have had you any time they wanted you."

"So who did they want?"

"Maybe me," he replied softly.

"Why you?"

"I don't want to talk about that," he said quickly. "Maybe tomorrow."

"What's so special about tomorrow?"

"I'm resigning tomorrow."

I gave him a long, hard look. "Don't do that."

"Maybe I need to do that."

"No you don't."

He showed me a quick smile then went on to join the

others. The coroner's people were preparing to remove the bodies of the slain officers.

So maybe Terry was just feeling tired of all this. Then again, maybe those L.A. cops had stumbled onto something he was simply unable to defend, and he was bowing to the inevitable.

God, I hoped not.

THE CHIEF AND I returned to Mammoth in virtual silence. We both had a lot to think about and it was obvious that he did not wish to say any more at the time regarding his surprising declaration that he was thinking about resigning. He was tired and out of sorts and I guess I was, too.

I wanted to ask him about the life and death of Vicki Douglas, also his relationship with Janice Sanford, but I had already drawn a strong reaction from that line of questioning and I knew better than to try it again at this particular moment. I really felt a bond with this guy but there were questions that needed answers and I felt that I was not serving that sense of friendship by not being straightforward with him. I also knew, however, that nothing would be gained by blustering through his defenses. Obviously there were things in his life that he did not wish to discuss. I have never been known as the "soul of tact," but it seemed more appropriate now to honor his sensitivities to every possible extent.

All the while, of course, I knew that there were many questions begging for answers and that the moment would come when absolute honesty between us would be the only way to keep that friendship intact.

It seemed, for example, that his relationship with Harley Sanford was woven in somehow with a sense of loyalty, or perhaps indebtedness, which may not be entirely seemly for a man in his position. I wanted to ask about that. Perhaps Terry owed his job to Harley Sanford. Politics, after all, form the lifeblood of many relationships; that did not have to be "dirty" but could be merely a proper sense of gratitude with no impropriety whatever.

On the other hand, many otherwise honorable men have been buried by that same misguided sense of gratitude. I would have preferred to know much more about the true relationship between Terry and Sanford; apparently only Terry himself could now enlighten me in that regard. I would have to wait for that. Meanwhile, there were other disturbing riddles commanding my attention.

First of all, the whereabouts of Janice Sanford and the particulars of her most recent brush with death.

Secondly, the whereabouts and present status of Tom Lancer. In that same connection, what was his relationship with Arthur Douglas, Vicki Douglas, Cindy Morgan, and perhaps even Martha Kaufman? For that matter, had there ever been more than a casual relationship with George Kaufman? How well had he known Vicki Douglas and Cindy Morgan? How well had he known Martha Kaufman? And how well did he really know Martha's mother? Was Janice Sanford intimately involved and in love with him as he implied? Was he really in love with her and on the verge of sweeping her up and carrying her off into the sunset?

How close had Chief Terry been to all these people and how many intimate connections could be drawn between them?

And why, really, was Terry now talking about resigning from his position in the community?

Why was Arthur Douglas shot and could this have had any bearing on his interest in me? If not, why had my home address and telephone number been found in this police officer's address book?

Who really had killed Vicki Douglas and what had been her relationship with the other victims? Had she really been a hooker?—if so, how would that figure into the grand scheme of things known?

Finally, why had Cindy Morgan left an urgent message for Arthur Douglas moments before he was shot and a short while before she was found murdered herself?

These were some of the questions that continued to bedevil me.

Terry dropped me at the hotel and said, "There you go, bud, thanks for the company."

"What company?" I asked him. "We haven't said two words the whole trip back."

"Sometimes that's the best company," he replied.

"Not for you, pal, not tonight. You've got heavy shit between your ears. What was that crap about resignation?"

"No crap. I'm just fed up."

I said, "No, I think you're running scared. Can't take the heat, huh?"

"Sure, screw you too, bud. Whoever said I had to spend the rest of my life behind this badge? Fuck it! Know how long it's been since I went fishing? Since I took a vacation? Since I took in a movie or went to a football game?"

I said, "Yeah, sure, my heart bleeds. Whoever said you needed to bury yourself out here in the sticks? A good cop like you could make it anywhere. So why did you settle for the sticks?"

"Careful there. You're talking about the sticks I love. Beats the hell out of anywhere you've ever lived."

I asked him, "So where do you go from here? Forest Service?—or maybe casino security or bouncing toughies at some bar? Stop it, you're breaking my heart. Come on, let's get serious."

This produced one of those characteristic swings in his mood. He chuckled. "Maybe I'll go to work in L.A."

I said, "You're too fucking old to be starting in L.A. Those kids down there would chew you up, and I'm not talking about the punks out on the street; I'm talking about the L.A. cops. They'd call you 'old timer' and short-sheet your patrol car every time you dozed off on graveyard—and those donut shops can be deadly at your age. So forget it."

"Nice thing about you, Joe," he replied, chuckling, "you cut right through the shit."

"So you're not retiring."

"I didn't say that."

"Say it, then. People in this town respect you and like you. They need you. More important, you need them. So let's hear no more of this retirement crap."

"It's not quite that easy."

"So who dirtied you?"

"Maybe I dirtied myself. I have to think about this,

Joe, but thanks. Maybe I'll have a different slant after some sleep."

We stared at each other silently for a moment then I asked, "Is it Janice?"

He exclaimed, "Jesus, you love to shoot from the hip, don't you."

"It is Janice, isn't it?"

He did not deny it or confirm it. But I knew, yeah. It was Janice.

# CHAPTER TWENTY-FIVE

I RAPPED LIGHTLY at the door and Marie opened it immediately, almost as though she had been poised there, awaiting my return. The time was wearing on to three o'clock so I was halfway surprised that she was waiting up for me.

She had changed into slinky lounging pajamas and she looked great. I stood at the door as I told her, "Took longer than I expected. Sorry. Just wanted to say good night properly. Figured you'd be sound asleep by now."

She said, "No, I knew you'd be back. Can you come in for a minute?"

I told her, "The whole town is asleep. Maybe we should be, too."

"I have fresh coffee."

"As a matter of fact, if it's okay, there is something on my mind. Can we talk?"

She swung the door wide as she replied, "That's why I made the coffee, dummy. Why so formal? Are you feeling embarrassed about this?"

I went on inside and took a seat at the table. "Couple of guys I knew died tonight. So if I'm acting like a jerk..."

"Of course not. I understand. Who died this time?"

"Two L.A. cops, Andrews and Zambrano. They were in town earlier tonight. Maybe you saw them."

She showed me a properly mournful face as she replied, "No, I guess not. How did they die?"

"They were shot. Up near Lee Vining."

"Why?"

"That's the question we'd all like to answer." I was suddenly feeling totally bombed out. Marie apparently saw it in my eyes. She hugged me warmly then went on to get the coffee. "It's crazy. Even in L.A., a crime wave of this dimension would be the talk of the town. I get the feeling that it has hardly gotten any attention here in Mammoth."

"Well, we just don't have Minicams and a television newsman on every corner. That doesn't mean that no one in town is aware of what's been going on. We have our own personal media here; it just spreads by word of mouth." She brought the coffee and sat down beside me. "Everybody in this town knows all about you by now."

I sipped the coffee, then replied, "God, Marie, I hope not *every*thing."

"Well, practically," she replied soberly.

It is strange how sometimes you can be totally blind and even ignorant regarding people who have been in your face for hours or even days. It is especially strange when you are the one who is blind but have always regarded yourself as a pretty sharp cop. I had just that moment noticed a bookcase directly opposite the table where I was sitting and not four feet away, stacked with psychology textbooks and other related subjects. Piled on the table, right beside my hand, was a collection of books by Los Angeles media psychiatrist David Viscott.

I must have been eyeing the collection with some interest because Marie asked me, "Do you listen to David?"

She was referring to a long-running series of television and radio programs in which the listening/viewing audience may directly consult the famed psychiatrist.

"Met the guy at a seminar once," I told her. "A friend of mine followed him around every chance she got. She wanted to go, so I went."

"So?"

"So what?"

"What did you think of him?"

"Brilliant guy," I said.

"That's an understatement, Joe. David Viscott is a full-blown genius. As a cop, you could learn a lot from David."

I said, "So send him over. I could use some genius right now. What would Viscott say about a guy like Harley Sanford?"

"My guess is that he would probably call Harley a dependent male who cannot or will not take responsibility for his own failures."

I said, "But he was a highly successful man."

"In some ways. In other ways, he was totally inadequate."

"Based on what?"

"Every womanizer is an inadequate male."

I smiled tiredly. "So where did you get such an interest in psychology?"

"I've studied it informally all my life."

"Why not formally?"

"I don't want to deal with other people's problems day

and night. That would take all the fun out of it."

"So what is your illumination on the problems between the sexes?"

"Too little honesty. Too many games."

"Both sexes?"

"Sure. A woman can be just as stupid as a man can be."

"And how about Janice Sanford?"

"She gave it away."

"Gave what away?"

"Her right to be herself."

"What if someone told you, right now, that Janice Sanford left town suddenly with another man?"

She replied, "I'd say good for her and long overdue."

"How do you think Harley would react to something like that?"

"Oh, he'd flip out for sure."

"Even though he has been playing around with other women steadily over the years?"

She said, "That is exactly why he would flip out. You have to understand something about men like him, Joe. Harley was totally dependent on Janice all these years. A psychiatrist would think of a woman like Janice as an 'enabler.' A man like Harley breeds on women like Janice because he is so inadequate within himself."

I said, "You should have gone for that degree."

"Well, don't take my word for it."

"I've thought of Harley as a totally controlling personality."

"Yes, he is. But, you know, that can be an overcompensation for an innate weakness."

I asked her, with a grin, "Are you going to bill me for this consultation?"

She gave me a solemn smile. "Depends on how tired you are, Joe. How tired are you?"

"Tired enough to die," I told her.

"Then you need a soothing massage. Take off your clothes and jump in the shower."

I said, "No you don't, kiddo. I have a feeling that your touch would put me out for the rest of the night."

"What could be so bad about that?"

"I think some people may be after my butt for real. You start that again and I might forget what I'm all about here."

She asked, "How long since you've slept?"

"I don't remember the last time I slept. Yesterday, maybe."

"You can't function long that way. What if I promise to be nice? I'll stand guard at your door as long as you say."

"That's a difficult offer to refuse but I really do have to get on my way. But I'll take you up on the use of your bathroom. I'd like to wet the face down a bit and see if that will revive me some."

"Sure. Whatever you'd like. How about if I cook us up some eggs?"

That sounded great to me. A brisk shower sounded even better but I was afraid that would have put me out for the night.

I was hungry, however, and there were other things still on my mind that I wanted to discuss with Marie before I left. So maybe a bite of food would serve both

needs. As it turned out, though, I would have been better
off to have left while I was still ahead.


I CAME OUT of the bathroom to the aromatic smell of
sizzling bacon. Marie announced cheerily, "Okay, Copp,
you made it just in time before disaster. Sit down and
belly up."

Beautifully basted eggs, crisp bacon, and English muf-
fins looked like anything but a disaster zone to me. It
was the best food I'd eaten in weeks—hell, maybe since
forever.

We ate with gusto and she seemed to be enjoying it
as much as I was. This woman had an appealing frank-
ness. In some, it could have been taken as brassiness or
impropriety. To me, it was charming directness. She
said, "Is this good, or what?"

I assured her. "It's damn good. Everything about you
has been good, Marie."

She watched me for a moment as I attacked the food,
then said, "So you're welcome to stay as long as you'd
like. In fact, if you don't have any problem with being
a kept man..."

I told her, with genuine warmth, "You're better than
that, kid, and worth a hell of a lot more than that."

She said, "So where have I gone wrong all these
years?"

"You were never married?"

"Oh, sure, I'm a three-time loser. So what has that
taught me?"

"Maybe it should have taught you to try, try again.

Or maybe—like me—it has taught you that marriage is often a great spoiler of romance. I've lost a few myself."

She said, "Yeah, you'd be a hard bastard to live with, I can see that. The problem for women, I think, is that we always try to tame the guy. Once we've succeeded in that, we can't stand his guts."

I said, "So you can't live with 'em and you can't live without 'em."

"I guess that's it," she said quietly. "Don't let me scare you off with this kind of stuff, Joe. I'm too old for you and you're too wild for me. But it could be fun for a while, couldn't it?"

"Already is."

"So let's just take it one day at a time."

"In my business, Marie, often we do not have the luxury of an entire day. Let's think of it as one moment at a time."

She replied soberly, "That's what we're doing, isn't it?"

I matched her sobriety as I said, "That's really all it ever is, Marie." We stared at each other quietly for a moment, then I asked, "How well did you know Martha?"

"How well did you know her?"

"Hardly at all."

"But well enough to marry her."

"I guess so. Have you heard about—?"

She did not give me a chance to mention that tragedy. "I heard all about it, yes. Everyone in town has heard about it. Hate to say this, Joe, but I'm afraid that all the sympathy has gone toward you."

"What does that mean?"

"Martha was not the most popular woman in this town, I'm afraid."

I did not know exactly how to respond. This had been the first negative comment I had ever heard concerning Martha. Maybe it set my nose just a bit because things began going downhill from that point. I asked her, "What are you getting at?"

"Nothing, I'm sorry. I had no right to ..."

I said, "No, I need to hear it."

She gave me a long solemn look before she replied, "You'll have to get that from someone else. Especially now. I'm sorry. I just can't talk about Martha."

"Can you talk about Cindy Morgan?"

"No."

"You didn't mind talking about her last night or the first time we met."

"It was different then."

"How was it different, then?"

"You can get this stuff from anybody. Sorry. You won't get it from me. You're too damned defensive."

That was a surprise to me. I hadn't realized that I was being defensive. So what the hell was that all about? I said, "You don't want to talk about Arthur Douglas either, do you?"

"No."

"Vicki Douglas?"

"Especially not her."

"She was found dead yesterday at Tahoe."

That shocked her. It took her a moment to reply, "That doesn't really surprise me. I'm sorry, but not surprised."

"Why not?"

"I guess I'm beyond surprise, after all the stuff that's happened around here."

I asked, "So nothing would surprise you?"

"Absolutely nothing," she replied soberly.

And obviously that was all she intended to say. We finished our coffee in an almost embarrassed silence.

After a moment she said quietly, "I have an early-morning call. Maybe you never sleep but I have to. So it's time to say goodnight. Last chance—would you like to stay?"

So what the hell had brought that sudden change to our warm rapport? Maybe she was just as tired as I was. I didn't know why, but I did know that it was over, at least for the moment. I said, "Thanks, but I really have to go."

There were secrets in this quiet town—dark secrets, it seemed. And maybe I would never plumb the full depths of that darkness.

# CHAPTER TWENTY-SIX

IT WAS PAST four o'clock when I again traversed the business district of Mammoth and made my way on through town. The streets were deserted and there was an almost ghostly feel to the night. A fine rain had developed against a typical windblown night, slanting in from the western peaks, not enough to soak the streets but potentially treacherous enough to drive with caution.

I wondered what the hell I had hoped to accomplish at such an hour in this sleeping town. Even the police department seemed tucked in for the night, as well as the hospital. I had been crazy, I decided, to leave the warm company of my friend at the hotel, and I immediately regretted doing so. This was the witching hour and there were not even any witches about to liven the night.

So I drove over to Martha's condo in the hope that something would show up among her possessions to give me a better focus on the developments of this case.

Or so I thought.

The telephone was ringing as I went inside. It was obviously Lancer's voice in taut response, but he did not give his name as he said, "Thank God, I've been trying

you every twenty minutes for hours. Don't identify
yourself. Do you understand the meaning of electronic
countermeasures?"

"Spook stuff," I replied. "Sure. Are you telling me I
need to check for that?"

"If you would, yes, please. Don't say anything else
until you're sure it's clean."

Well, what the hell?—I didn't have any gear with me
to check out stuff like that. Electronic surveillance is a
very sophisticated business, the way it has evolved these
days, but I tried the usual games to look for hidden bugs
in the obvious places for a couple of minutes before
reporting back, "Looks clean enough, but don't trust it
to anything really important. What's going on?"

"Don't use any names."

"Gotcha, no names."

"A certain person desperately needs your counsel. Can
you meet us?"

"Just tell me where."

"You remember our first meeting?"

"The very first?"

"Right. I'll be there for at least the next twenty minutes. Please come."

"I'll be there."

"Alone. My friend would be very nervous if anyone
else came with you. So would I."

"I'd like to bring John with me."

"*Especially* not him."

I said quietly, "Gotcha. I'm on my way. Look for me."

"You can't miss me," he said, and hung up on that
note.

Curiouser and curiouser, yeah. Lancer's "friend" was

Janice Sanford, of course, and the first time I'd met Lancer was at the Mammoth airport. Why meet there? It had not been the safest harbor in the world the last time I'd seen that place.

But it was not my game, it was just my play.

And I had to assume that the guy knew why he needed to play it this way. But what did he know about Chief Terry that I did not? That was a worry, yeah...it was a worry.

THE NIGHT HAD worsened a bit in the airport area, the wind more blustery and the rain considerably heavier in spots. The higher peaks to the west were largely obscured by a fast-moving weather front and it seemed probable that those areas were encountering at least a dusting of snowfall. It was definitely raining here now, enough so that you would not wish to be caught in it without some protection.

I did not see Lancer or his car but a small team of mechanics were working on the Cessna jet inside a hangar. It seemed an odd hour to find these guys so involved, but what did I know? I supposed that it was logical enough to find them there, though, if Lancer was pushing the repair toward a quick conclusion. That could explain his request to meet him at the airport.

The chief mechanic greeted me in the open doorway of the hangar. "Can I help you, sir?"

I explained that I was meeting Lancer.

"Are you Mister Copp?" he asked.

"Yeah."

"Could I see some I.D.?"

I showed him my driver's license. He inspected it with more than a perfunctory examination, smiled, then produced a sealed, handwritten letter from a back pocket of his uniform.

"He's not here?" I asked.

"No, sir."

"When did he leave the note?"

"About . . . oh, several hours ago."

"Several *hours* ago?"

"Yes, sir."

"He delivered it personally?"

"Yes, sir."

I thanked the mechanic and he went back to his work while I read the note from Lancer. This guy, I decided—speaking of Lancer—was playing it super cagey. I remembered that I had concluded that he had come from some kind of military background. So maybe the guy was just playing it overly cautious—and certainly there had been plenty of reason for that, but this was sounding like something from a spy novel.

The note from Lancer read, in bold, flowing script, "The South Tufas, any hour on the hour. Come alone or not at all."

I could not call this paranoia, not in view of all that had gone down over the past few days, but it did seem to be a bit more dramatic than necessary. What the hell, it was his life at stake and perhaps that of the woman he loved—so how could I fault it?

Problem was, I was having a bit of trouble deciphering it. The "Tufas" no doubt referred to the large, towering formations at Mono Lake, which is in the same general region where the two cops from L.A. had died just hours earlier. The lake itself is approximately thirteen miles long by eight miles wide. The tufa towers dot the shoreline primarily along the west and south shores in an essentially wild, uninhabited area.

Mono Lake's landscape has been shaped over millions of years by volcanic activity that also produced many craters in and near the lake, and the tufa towers dramatically enhance the sense of its ancient past. The last of these craters erupted only six hundred years ago, and the numerous hot springs and steam vents in the Mono basin show us that volcanic activity is still present.

The tufa, or sinter, as it is sometimes called, is produced as a concretionary sediment of calcium carbonate. The unusual formations occur when calcium-bearing freshwater springs well up through the alkaline lake water, which is rich in carbonates. Calcium and carbonate precipitate out as limestone. In time, a tower forms around the mouth of the underwater spring. The lake level has dramatically receded, exposing these ancient towers far above the water line.

The level of Mono Lake has dropped approximately forty feet and doubled its salinity in the past several decades. This is due to the city of Los Angeles, several hundred miles away, diverting the Sierra streams that feed the lake. It is perhaps worth noting that this has grown to be an increasingly unpopular diversion by local citizens and environmentalists alike.

Throughout the lake's long existence, salts and minerals have washed into the lake from the several mountain streams, and because it has no outlet, as the freshwater evaporates the salts are left behind. The lake is now about two and a half times as salty and eighty times as alkaline as seawater.

Though called a "dead sea" by some, it abounds with life, and the lake is ecologically vital to several important species, which take much of their sustenance from the food chain originating in the lake—green algae, brine shrimp, and the brine fly. An estimated four trillion shrimp commonly swim in Mono's water. They are thought to belong to a unique species that has particularly adapted to the special conditions there. The shrimp and flies provide food for more than eighty species of migratory birds, many of which nest at the lake.

Of course my earlier characterization of this lake as a "moonscape" refers only to my impression of the strange landscape features and the eerie quality of the surroundings. One could even imagine such a time during the youth of our Moon when it could have looked exactly this way, had life been present there.

I was not looking forward to another run up the highway in this steadily worsening weather, and certainly I had no desire to invade unfamiliar territory at such a time. I was feeling a bit cranky, too, over Lancer's theatrics, which seemed to be creating an unnecessary problem. But I also could not abandon the guy and especially not Janice Sanford's problems, real or imagined.

I was a bit testy, too, over Lancer's desire to exclude John Terry's participation. Not that I was feeling particularly uneasy about the meeting but because I felt like a "stranger in a strange land" and I would have preferred to have the assistance of an expert guide. But let me lay it out level; I was aggravated, really, because Lancer seemed to be impugning Terry's reliability and I had bought this cop all the way. Not that I had accepted the Chief unquestionably all the way, but I had not really been that ambivalent about the man and I guess I saw Lancer's comment as theatrics rather than caution.

Also, of course, let's be realistic about this, I would not be much of a cop if I had not been aware throughout this experience that my life was in jeopardy, and perhaps extreme jeopardy. If I was going to be blindly skulking about on a stormy night, I would have felt a lot more comfortable with John Terry backing me up instead of Tom Lancer. Lancer had shown himself to be a ready enough man with a gun but I sure as hell would have preferred the demonstrated expertise of John Terry if the need arose.

Almost as though to echo my own dark thoughts, as I left the airport I noticed a car parked beside the road just above the point where the airport proper joins the Owens River Road, which is where I had intercepted one of the gunmen following the attack on the plane. The rain was beginning to pelt down and my visibility was not that sharp, but I thought on reflection moments later that I recognized that vehicle.

It looked, I decided in afterthought, very much like one of the cars used by the Mammoth police.

Sure, I had just been complaining that I would have liked to have Terry along for the ride. But not, I think, this way.

The lousy suspicions surfacing inside of me were all I needed to make my night complete.

As I peeled out onto Highway 395 and began the run north toward Mono Lake, I was positive that I saw that same car slip discreetly behind me.

So okay. The more the merrier.

# CHAPTER TWENTY-SEVEN

According to my map, access to the South Tufa area is gained along State Highway 120, which intersects U.S. Highway 395 about five miles south of Lee Vining. The turnoff eastward at that point is a well-marked road. Actually, Highway 120 provides direct access westward from Highway 395 to Yosemite National Park via Tioga Pass and is a popular route during summer, often impassable during winter. The eastern leg of this state highway ends about forty miles later at Benton, where U.S. 6 winds on through Nevada. It is a lonely and little-traveled road, almost like a route to nowhere.

I felt as if I had already been "nowhere." Even U.S. 395 was sparsely traveled at this time of night. If someone indeed was tailing me, he was skillfully concealed, which could not have been too difficult under the circumstances. The rain had slackened off but it was being replaced by a penetrating fog that alternately raised and lowered in a sometimes disturbing pattern—which simply means that now and then I was encountering dense fog at "ground zero."

I had really begun experiencing slow going at the point where I left Highway 395 and started the incursion into the South Tufa area. This is a lonely road at best; in the dense fog, it was almost surrealistic at times, even to the point that I was experiencing occasional periods of vertigo. If someone was following me now, I could only wish him luck. The guy would almost have had to know my destination to be keeping up with me under these conditions.

Actually I had not been sure at any point that I was being followed from the airport. As the night wore on, I found myself growing less and less sure of anything. The weather was doing a number on me, and I was becoming more and more irritated with Lancer for setting the meeting in this impossible spot. Surely, I thought, he could have come up with a more reasonable place to meet.

Time has a way of getting out of sync when the physical perceptions are clouded. I had become quite an expert on that kind of shaded reality because I had been living, more or less, in that particular mode throughout this experience. So my railing against the problem was something like a blind man complaining that his glasses were dirty. The sensation here was the equivalent of finding yourself completely cut off from everything that is real, yet knowing that you must not give in to panic if you intend to prevail.

What should have been an easy half-hour run from the airport had now consumed more than an hour and I was still battling the night. That realization was no doubt responsible for my lousy frame of mind. My map was showing a distance of something like five miles to the South Tufa turnoff and then less than a mile to the parking area near the shoreline. So it was roughly the same as trying to land an airplane onto an unknown, unlighted, and fog-shrouded landing strip, with nothing more than an odometer to measure my progress.

The only consolation, if you could call it that, was the realization that it would be just as difficult for Lancer to find the place as it was for me. I almost felt like yelling aloud into the night, "There, damn you. Set it up better next time." But of course I didn't do that. I was supposed to be a responsible person involved in a possibly life-threatening situation, so I was trying to keep my cool.

So it was a great comfort when my difficult progress was finally rewarded by a dim marker along the road pointing the entrance to the South Tufa area. I almost missed it, and maybe I would have eventually wound up in Nevada if I had not been diligently counting the ticks on my odometer.

I was not sure that I had found the right spot until I nosed into the parking area. Another car was there. A personalized license plate identified the owner as "SKYJOCK."

It was Lancer's car, sure.

But where was the "Skyjock" himself? Except for a few prairie dogs, there was not a living soul in evidence.


THE ONLY REDEEMING feature of this desolate night was the realization that somewhere up there the day was beginning to dawn, evidenced only by a somewhat lighter cast to the darkness. The fog here was exhibiting a peek-a-boo effect as it swirled in almost rhythmic patterns around this ancient landscape. It was windy and cold enough to encourage me to seek warmth from an old leather jacket that I kept folded into the rear of the van.

As I was donning the jacket, a gust of brightness in the fog attracted my attention to Lancer's car. The right side had been splashed with fresh road tar. A closer look revealed that the front tire was covered with that gunk. I tried to look inside the car to investigate further but both doors were locked and I could discern nothing of special interest through the windows in the darkness. The guy could have picked that stuff up anywhere, of course, but I make a living by noticing such seemingly innocuous things. I returned to my van and belted on the holstered Beretta beneath the jacket.

The path from the parking area to the lakeshore was enveloped in billowing fog carried by the gusty wind, and though I had visited this area some years back, it had been brief and memorable only because of the weird limestone formations present; the rest of it was essentially forgotten. I did recall the long walk from the parking lot to the water, and this time I was happy to have the jacket because the combination of the fog and still-threatening rain could have been quite uncomfortable without it.

I presumed that Lancer and Janice would be expecting me to meet them somewhere in the vicinity of the tufa, though this was making less and less sense as I went along. I would have thought that they would be waiting for me in the car. But with the guy so obviously into theatrics, perhaps that would explain their willingness to wait for me in a less desirable spot. I could not imagine even the prairie dogs enjoying this enshrouding gloom.

* * *

Someone was walking ahead of me on the trail. I did not see anyone or otherwise encounter any other human presence except for a muffled footstep now and then, obviously pacing me at a steady distance. I did not like this game. I called out softly, "Lancer!"

The footsteps paused when I did, advanced when I did, and kept the game going all the way along while the only response to my call was the barking cries of the nearby prairie dogs.

It is a long walk along that path. The visibility was not all that bad, except in fast-moving patches of fog. The skies were gradually becoming lighter and even drier. Though still not entirely ideal, at least there was some continuing improvement over the night. The wind remained a problem, though not severe, due to its effect on the fog. In this case the fog was actually moisture-laden surface-based clouds, which were being driven horizontally by the wind.

I could see enough to know that I was advancing into the dry, ancient lakebed itself. The tufa is spread throughout this area, some fully exposed on dry land, here and there, but also many standing in spires rising high above the waterline, like so many sand castles or wrecked ships forever waiting for rescue by forces beyond the memory of modern man.

I spotted a fog-shrouded figure moving behind a field of tufa as I neared the beach area. Almost as a warning, I heard the screeching of the gulls flying above me. I called out again, "Lancer!"

"Over here," a female voice replied faintly.

Well, that was not Lancer. Janice, maybe—but where was Lancer?

I heard it again. "Joe," softly.

I was advancing on the sound, but it too seemed to be elusively shifting with the wind. That voice—it sounded like Janice, but then again maybe not. It was a voice I knew, yet one from some dim recess of my mind.

What was giving me trouble here was an almost strobelike effect produced by the rapidly alternating rise and fall of the shifting fog, as though the fog itself was a living presence superimposing itself upon the movements and the sounds of this stark environment.

The woman called to me again, almost as though summoning me like a chorus of sea sirens of antiquity, luring unsuspecting seamen to their doom.

I did not feel like an ancient mariner but I knew I was in trouble. It scared the hell out of me and gave me a shiver when I unsuspectingly stepped into a shallow lagoon and a small animal, which I never actually saw, skittered against my ankle. I froze, one foot in the lagoon and maybe the other on the moon for all I knew.

The "Harpie" called me again and this time I saw her clearly for a split second.

My heart froze.

This was not Janice Sanford.

This woman wore short-cropped dark hair, taller than Janice, younger than Janice.

It was not Janice.

The fog-shrouded figure was my own dear Martha—unless I was totally crazy, and I was not so sure that I was not.

There was a level of insanity and disbelief closing in

on me and I had to wonder if my mind was playing tricks on me—or was Janice, Lancer, or even Martha herself truly present and playing deadly games with me?

Deadly, for sure. The "Harpie" had a small pistol trained on me.

Had I, in my obsession to find my own truth, placed myself in ultimate jeopardy in this surreal "human-scape" of shifting realities?

Dante's inferno? Not really. Copp's inferno.

# CHAPTER TWENTY-EIGHT

**T**HE CONFLICTS WITHIN me were enormous. On one subtle level of stark truth, the real Martha had a real gun pointed at me. On another level, all was suspect and I was having trouble discerning the real from the unreal during this time-compressed moment in that strangest of strange lands.

She called softly, "Joe, we could have had it all. Why did you have to be such a damn fool?"

This was sort of like a conversation with a being who did not really exist. I recognized the voice, sure—it was Martha, okay—and even the words sounded like something that I may have heard her say to me before, but the whole thing was hitting me with such devastating authenticity that I could not deny the reality of the experience.

I had lived through this scene before.

I croaked, "Do you want to kill me *again*, Martha?"

She replied hollowly, "You should have stayed dead, Joe. Look at the mess we're all in now."

"Speak for yourself, kid. How many people have you killed this week?"

She was moving again with the goddamned foglike strobes playing a tattoo across my face. But her gun had not wavered. It seemed that she was trying to get a better angle on me as she said, "Nobody would have had to die except for your overpoweringly sanctimonious police mentality. Who ever told you that you were supposed to protect the world from sin? I didn't kill those people, Joe. *You* killed them."

I was thunderstruck. I remembered this girl, now, and her special talents with firearms. She had been a champion in college on the rifle range. To quote her own characterization, she could "shoot a flea off a dog's butt without touching the dog." I had seen the trophies that proved it. I asked her, "So why didn't you just get it over with the first time and save us all this trouble?"

"I tried to, Joe. Why didn't you cooperate?"

"Did Harley cooperate?"

"That was difficult, yes, but he started it all. He was going to leave my mother broke and humiliated."

At last I was coming alive again. I knew her game, now. She was trying to set me up for a clear, killing shot. I knew how to play that game, too. I kept warily circling like a wounded wolf reluctant to abandon his prey. I said, "That doesn't wash, Martha. You didn't do this for your mother. Unless you want me to believe that you gave her a hotshot just to salve her pride. Where is she, by the way?"

"She's safe. Do you think I'm some kind of monster that I'd be willing to kill my own mother?"

We were still playing the waiting game—and I was still worried about Lancer. Could she have already decided that he had become too dangerous a liability—like me? Or was he lurking about the tufa waiting for an opportune shot, too?

The sudden roar of her gun was not even enough to totally dislodge my sense of suspended animation. I just stood there and blinked as a piece of tufa, shattered by her bullet, hit me in the face like a razor cut. Still I was frozen as the blood trickled down my cheek. I suppose I would have died there if John Terry had not snapped me out of it by a shout from behind.

"Joe, dammit, wake up!"

Terry's warning not only woke me up, it shocked me out of my stupor and also distracted Martha enough to give me an opportunity to defend myself. In the freeze-frame unfoldment of the moment, I instinctively flung myself behind a clump of grotesque limestone. Finally, the realization was exploding all over me—a hundred million clip-flashes of Martha trying to take me out in L.A., and the reenactment now of that murderous intent.

Almost as a sequence in slow motion, Tom Lancer rose up out of the fog like a murderous apparition with his pistol raised and ready, no more than ten yards from Martha's position. Had he been backing her up all the way through this charade? I was clawing for the Beretta even while Lancer's pistol was taking my range. John Terry, standing ankle-deep in the shallow lagoon, beat me to the punch. His big .357 roared once, eclipsing the lighter reports from Martha's now-frantic fire. Lancer was out of action. Martha was not and she was still trying to bracket me.

So fuck this shit.

I had never laid down for any man; and I sure as hell wasn't going to do so for Martha again, no matter how insane it had all become.

I sprung the Beretta from its holster without even

thinking about it and squeezed off a single round. Nothing fancy, no grandstanding or trick shooting for the press box, I simply squeezed off a round.

And Martha died again, this time for real.

But it hurt...just as bad the second time around.

Copp was in shock no more, but somehow I almost wished I were.

# CHAPTER TWENTY-NINE

**W**ELL ... SO THIS was the week that never should have been—but was.

Martha had died but once, of course. The body that I identified in the morgue in Los Angeles and that same body that we brought home in the Sanford jet was Vicki Douglas all along—the "unlucky hooker" whose body I discovered later in Sanford's Tahoe home. That was a daring identity switch—and must have felt, at the time, like a brilliant stroke. The goal was twofold: not only to confuse the real identity of the corpse in Los Angeles but also to further implicate Harley Sanford in the woman's apparent death in Tahoe and to suggest that she had been murdered in Sanford's bed.

The unfortunate funeral home attendant who picked up "Martha's" body at the airport in Mammoth had been reported missing and later found dead in a wilderness area outside Bridgeport. He had been the victim of a lethal "hotshot" of the same narcotic substance found in Janice Sanford's bloodstream on the morning of her brush with death.

But this is a "cute" one: Sanford's cartoon character "tough guys," Sammy and Clifford, who were found dead beneath the cold waters of Lake Tahoe, had been dispatched in an identical manner, except that—and here's the cute part—the investigating officers at Tahoe found evidence that their injections were administered by lethal darts apparently shot from a tranquilizer gun.

I have to give full credit for this deadly wrinkle to Martha. Her co-conspirator, Tom Lancer, had the perfect alibi, himself hospitalized in Mammoth with a self-inflicted flesh wound incurred during the airport shoot-out.

The whole purpose of that airport shootout was to destroy the body of Martha's substitute, Vicki Douglas, so Martha could surface later, feign ignorance, and reclaim her legacy. Maybe it even would have worked except for a couple of bad breaks.

Positive identification of mutilated gunshot victims is an iffy business at best in a morgue setting, before cosmetic restoration by an undertaker. Martha and Vicki Douglas were about the same size and build, with similar hairstyles, so it is not too remarkable that the deception had not been immediately apparent. Of course, the truth no doubt would have been discovered at some point, which is why both Martha and Lancer were so intent upon destroying that corpse before it could be returned for normal burial in the home environment. Even though I had twice viewed the body in the Los Angeles morgue, the rapid deterioration by the time I last viewed that body—plus the unnatural appearance normally encountered among the dead—made it very unlikely that I would have discovered the ruse even with my full memory in place.

When Janice Sanford's original plan for claiming her daughter's body in Los Angeles—under Lancer's watchful eye—went awry and I, as the legal claimant, had to be called in to identify the body, Martha and Lancer were forced to play it by ear from that point. Lancer had already sent in the "soldier of fortune" imports and it must have seemed a simple matter to destroy the body in a fiery inferno at the airport with no danger to Lancer and with only the funeral home attendant as a witness to Lancer's version of events. With Janice and I aboard the plane, it called for more improvisation on Lancer's part—an "Academy Award"–winning performance of being under fire and even winged by the bogus assassins. He fooled me as well as Chief Terry.

These poor bastards thought they were hired for an easy arson job on the plane. As it turned out, they became pawns in the bigger game when Janice and I unexpectedly accompanied the body from Los Angeles. These guys were sacrificial goats in the largest sense; one of them did not even know how to drive the stolen getaway vehicle.

If all that seems too bizarre, imagine how panicky it must have been for the conspirators when the whole thing began unraveling like a loose ball of yarn when I survived the attempt on my life in Los Angeles and returned to Mammoth.

Of course, I was never supposed to live to return from L.A., and the entire quirky chain of circumstances would not have developed if I had simply died like a nice boy when I was supposed to.

It may be understandable, then, why Martha was so upset with me for spoiling their grand plot.

It all began when George Kaufman, several years earlier, started keeping his own clandestine records of Harley Sanford's illegal wheeling and dealing, not only at the casino but also of Sanford's other business interests. This could have been for Kaufman's own protection as well as possible blackmail.

Sanford was totally corrupt and had been bilking partners and clients alike for years. His entire financial empire had been built around illegal and dishonest pursuits all of his life. Martha had known of some of this, perhaps from her first husband, Kaufman, but also maybe in some measure by her own direct knowledge.

That could account for Kaufman's "suspicious death" two years earlier, but that is pure conjecture on my part. It must have been devastating enough for Martha when she discovered that her own father had deliberately set her up in a disastrous marriage with his partner in crime, who was also homosexual.

These things have a way of leveling themselves out; it may have made it much easier for her, later, to involve herself in plots against her own father and ultimately to kill him. Of such twisted convolutions are heinous crimes often inspired. We should all remember that when seeking to manipulate others.

Martha's initial motivation undoubtedly had been to save her mother from financial ruin and public humiliation—perhaps even from becoming legally liable for her husband's criminal pursuits. This guy was *rotten*— and Martha knew it.

When she learned of Harley's diversion of company funds and secret Swiss accounts, coupled with his plan to run away with his lover—Cindy Morgan, one of her closest friends—something must have snapped in this woman.

It should also be worth noting that she was later described by another close acquaintance as "her father's daughter," suggesting that her venal predilections were inherited to some degree. I have revealed earlier that both Vicki Douglas's mother in Carson City and Marie here in Mammoth held low opinions of the Sanford clan.

I had been inclined to discount much of that to sour grapes or other personal motives, but sometimes it may be true that evidence of smoke is also evidence of fire.

The computer diskette obtained from Martha's safety-deposit box contained a damning record of all of Harley's financial shenanigans, including his secret Swiss account numbers, which gave her access to manipulation and transfer of millions. That is what had the man in such a sweat from the moment he discovered that Martha had possession of it all.

Then when his million bucks in bearer bonds disappeared, he became unglued and went after his daughter. That explains the torching of the gallery and the burglary of Martha's condo by Sanford's hired thugs, although it is also possible that the torch job was simple, bald intimidation.

I don't know how really to explain a guy like Tom Lancer. It would be too easy to account for his behavior here as a simple matter of "raging adventurism." It had to go deeper than that. When he was recruited by Martha he was willing without apparent restraint to involve himself in vile intrigues.

Maybe it was exciting for him—or maybe it was simple greed that finally pushed his button over the edge. Evidently he loved the game. He will have several decades to wonder about that, himself, if he does not draw the death penalty for these intrigues.

I cannot explain why the guy came up with the fictional love affair with Janice Sanford except to make himself look innocent and throw me off in case things went sour as their plot unfolded. Janice was undeniably shocked and distressed when I asked her about his reputed love affair with her.

So why the outrageous attacks on Harley Sanford? This went beyond simple murder. Several times they had tried to set him up on murder charges, and when that did not succeed, his death must have seemed like the only recourse.

In human history, these are the truly dark moments of the soul. Patricide is not as rare as it may seem, but it is always ugly to encounter it, whatever the motive. Perhaps the easiest answer is simple greed, but in a complex situation like this one, the pat answer is seldom the right one.

A whole phalanx of criminal charges were ripe and awaiting exposure at every turn, at every moment, so this was obviously not a master plan woven of a single piece but rather a succession of crisis-point adjustments requiring constant attempts to plug the holes in this sieve-like conspiracy.

After all is said and done, maybe it all does come down to simple greed, power, and ruthless opportunism running wild.

The street shooting of Officer Arthur Douglas in Mammoth was probably set up by Martha and Lancer initially to get Douglas out of the picture and frame

Harley for his murder in the bargain. They knew that Douglas was getting too close to the truth. If Harley's machinations were exposed, they would be exposed and their entire plot would become meaningless.

Arthur Douglas was no dummy. In his statement given after his recovery in the hospital, he explained that he had been aware of Cindy Morgan's interest in Harley Sanford and had learned that she was planning on leaving the country with him. He suspected that Sanford was connected to the mob and was absconding with illegal money from his business interests. He was a friend of the girl and wanted to protect her. His interest in me, evidenced by my mention in his personal address book, was related to my association with Martha. He sensed that Martha was somehow involved in a conspiracy with her father.

Lancer has already made a plea bargain in Officer Douglas's attempted murder. He admitted renting a silver Continental and doing the actual shooting. He also confessed to hiring the two assassins in the follow-up attempt on Douglas's life in the hospital.

One of the worst miscalculations of these two was their failing to recognize the capabilities of a small-town cop like John Terry. If he had not been at the hospital that day, perhaps little of this plot would ever have been brought to light.

Now the conspirators were in a hell of a sweat. According to Lancer's own statement, Cindy Morgan was the most dangerous threat to Sanford's millions. She was marked for death in any event, since she knew too much about Harley's business. The whole conspiracy could have come unraveled with the real possibility that Sanford had confided in her about everything—or the fear that he would do so.

Still using the rented Continental, Lancer lured the already panicky Sanford into a meeting near the ski resort at Mammoth Mountain. He and Martha ambushed the Sanford car—targeting only Cindy and allowing Harley to escape. Evidently there was still a spark of decency left in Martha, as she was reluctant to kill her father outright at this point. Lancer claimed that Martha was totally responsible—that she shot the girl cold and told her father, "Now maybe you'll leave me alone. Consider yourself lucky that I'm not sending one of these between your eyes. You're finished, Dad." They then drove away, leaving the dazed man wondering what to do next.

It is therefore perhaps understandable that Sanford simply abandoned the car in a makeshift hideout off the road and fled the scene on foot. This poor bastard was in a state of shock such as I could understand.

Lancer claimed in a sworn statement that Martha had been present during the staged attack at the airport and when that plan failed, she was in a state of desperation and again forced to improvise. She followed the hearse to Bridgeport and boldly presented herself at the mortuary as a family member. She held a gun on the attendant and forced him to prepare a closed-casket order to which she forged my name. Then she had him weigh and seal an empty coffin identified as Martha Kaufman. The attendant was ordered to carry Vicki's body, still in the body bag, and place it in the trunk of her car for transport to her father's home at Tahoe. She then administered a lethal "hotshot" to the attendant and dumped his body in a wilderness area near Bridgeport.

And this was the "soft...wistful...vulnerable" girl that I had married.

Martha herself, according to Lancer and verified by Janice, supplied the "hotshot" to her mother when she became hysterical after Martha revealed herself and the plot against her father, actually believing that she could persuade her mother to go along with the insanity.

I feel that Martha only intended to "control" her mother, not to kill her.

Knowing that the jig was up, Lancer told us where to find the "tranquil" mother in a small cabin in the June Lake area near Lee Vining.

God only knows, and I don't want to know, what would have been Martha's final answer to the problem with Janice had they succeeded in carrying out their plan.

I believe that the burglary at the Sanford home while Janice was in the hospital was a setup by Martha or Lancer to cover their own tracks in case it became necessary to kill Janice. Just for the record, it seems to me that all the other burglaries were inspired by the search for Sanford's missing goods and committed by Sammy and Clifford, acting under Sanford's orders.

Andrews and Zambrano, the crack L.A. sheriff's detectives, were probably the unluckiest bastards of all. They were within a heartbeat of breaking this case. Lancer, the consummate ex-military "spook," had highly sophisticated electronic surveillance gear in his car and had been monitoring the local police frequencies as well as all telephone transmissions in and out of the police department. This enabled him to intercept Andrews' and

Zambrano's conversations with Chief Terry and other police personnel.

He knew that they were en route to Tahoe in an attempt to match the Tahoe body with the victim who they had I.D.'d in Los Angeles. This would have blown the whole plot wide open, establishing conclusive proof that Vicki Douglas, not Martha Kaufman, had died in Los Angeles, and that a deliberate misidentification had been criminally engineered.

These cops were sharp enough to realize, or at least to suspect, that two victims of the same approximate age and time of death—both related in some way to Sanford and me—could be closely connected. And of course these guys had personally viewed the victim in Los Angeles. In the cabin where Janice was found safely sedated, we discovered the L.A. deputies' case file containing photos, fingerprints, and their notes on the Los Angeles murder victim. Their notes indicated that they had interviewed several Mammoth acquaintances of Martha Kaufman.

Lancer knew that their game was just about up. What else did they have to lose from another killing or two? They had to keep the game going. This ambush was intended to plug another hole in this rapidly disintegrating plot.

It is ironic, perhaps, that the "brilliant stroke" with the identity switch at Tahoe would have been their master coup had not the L.A. cops decided to investigate what must have seemed to them to be a long shot. Martha and Lancer actually had no other recourse but to kill the deputies once the body switch had gone forward and the deputies had become suspicious.

I save this for last because it is the most painful part for me to recount. Betrayal is always a particularly bitter pill; to be betrayed by love with one's own life in the balance is the bitterest pill of all, especially when one feels like a sap in the bargain. Perhaps there had been something approximating love when Martha and I began, but Martha's "love" was of a far different character than my definition of love. I have to believe that her interest in me from the outset was largely motivated by her desire to manipulate me. Her almost insane determination to best her father was the driving force of her life and perhaps had been so for a very long time.

If I had not been so blinded by the impact of my first meeting with her, perhaps I would have seen the character flaws that quickly led to her destruction—and of course very nearly my own. As it worked out, I had become very disturbed by her apparent obsession over her problems with Harley, but by that time I had begun working on a form of obsession myself: to make our love real, and special, and forever—little knowing that her interests would take me in directions that I could not possibly tolerate. On the very night of our honeymoon, she was already beginning to spew vile accusations against her father and trying to enlist my help in furthering her own sense of "justice." And of course I did not know at the time about the bearer bonds or any of the other intrigues that were driving Harley Sanford nuts.

Martha "enlisted" me, perhaps in the same way that she had already enlisted Lancer. I did not know at that time the value of the bearer bonds or that they were Harley Sanford's property. I only knew, or believed, that something valuable was in the safety-deposit box and that Harley was trying to get it away from her.

The torching of the gallery was the first concrete evidence I had seen that some sort of "war" was going on between father and daughter—and Martha had been very careful to keep me at a distance from her parents. So I have to feel that the whole deadly plot had been brewing in her mind from my first meeting with her.

So, yeah, I was carefully set up. I had been led to believe that Martha was being pursued by her own father and that she was fearful for her life. I was taking her home with me. Vicki Douglas supposedly was in about the same fix as Martha and she was planning to stay with us in Southern California while seeking a new life for herself. Yes, Martha had told me that Vicki had become involved in prostitution under Sanford's influence and that she felt a responsibility to "rescue" the girl.

Some rescue.

By the time we were within a short distance of my place near L.A., I finally began to understand what Martha was asking of me. She wanted me to assist her in an outrageous plot against her father. We started arguing and I pulled the car over to have it out with her. Before I realized what was happening she had pulled my gun out of the glove box and shot me without warning. I cannot speak to my sense of betrayal and dismay but I know that it was more than a mere gunshot wound that propelled me into this hideous encounter with extreme shock.

I am still a bit fuzzy about the struggle itself and the actual chain of events. The only way that I can reconstruct the actual sequence is that Vicki ran terrified from the car after I was shot and Martha pursued her and killed her with my gun. Some of this I have learned from Lancer, who was following my car at a discreet distance. According to Lancer, Martha placed her wedding band on the dead girl's finger and dropped her engraved cigarette lighter in the pocket of Vicki's jeans. Thinking that I was dead, they stripped the car of the girls' luggage and personal effects. In their haste to get away, Martha's bracelet came loose and was later found by the police near Vicki's body.

I guess I came to, moments later, and somehow was able to drive the few blocks to my house, although apparently banging up the car along the way.

It could have worked. All of it or any of it could have worked. Only God knows why it did not, certainly not me. This could have been set in any small town, anywhere in the world. All of the principals in this adventure knew one another, yet we all must be aware that no human being truly knows others in the recesses of their own hearts and minds.

WE DID BURY the real Martha Kaufman-Copp in a closed coffin, not because the body was so disfigured but because the soul itself was. Janice would not allow a viewing of her monster-child.

It is amazing, though, how quickly the threads of a life can come back together following a tragedy. Chief Terry did not rethink his decision to resign from the force. He will be leaving as soon as a suitable replacement has been appointed. For my money, there will never be a replacement for this cop.

He is going to be a very busy man, nevertheless. Janice Sanford has prevailed upon him to take over the management of her many properties and she will need a lot of help picking up the pieces of that shattered empire. I did not envy him the task of unraveling the legalities of that million bucks in bearer bonds and the Swiss accounts. I know of no more worthy a man than him for that role. It is my guess, and hope, that love is already blossoming between those two and that the horrors of yesterday shall quickly become no more than the faded memory of a distant nightmare. So be it—and I will be looking forward to one day cracking another "short dog" of Jack Daniels with this superlative man. That is from the heart, "bud."

As for myself, I run into Mammoth a lot more often these days. Have a good pal up there and she has no peer in the whole state when it comes to making a man feel like a real king, at least for a day—or a night, for that matter. Besides, I need to pursue my new interest in human psychology.

Above all, I have developed a new respect for the mere joy of being alive and enjoying the company of nice people and good friends. But I should tell you that the first thing I did upon returning to the sanctuary of my home in Southern California was to place a classified ad in the Los Angeles *Times* reading: FOR SALE—ONE EXPENSIVE PAINTING, TITLED "GOD'S COUNTRY," FREE TO FIRST CALLER.